HARLEM'S AWAKENING
Peppur Chambers

ISBN-13: 978-0615932026
ISBN-10: 0615932029

Edited by Lilliam Rivera
Artwork by Benjamin Mills

Printed in the U.S.A.

BLACK HILL PRESS
blackhillpress.com

Black Hill Press is a publishing collective founded on collaboration. Our growing family of writers and artists are dedicated to the novella—a distinctive, often overlooked literary form that offers the focus of a short story and the scope of a novel. We believe a great story is never defined by its length.

Our independent press produces uniquely curated collections of Contemporary American Novellas. We also celebrate innovative paperback projects with our Special Editions series. Books are available in both print and digital formats, online and in your local bookstore, library, museum, university gift shop, and selected specialty accounts. Discounts are available for book clubs and teachers.

Contemporary American Novellas
1. Corrie Greathouse, *Another Name for Autumn*
2. Ryan Gattis, *The Big Drop: Homecoming*
3. Jon Frechette, *The Frontman*
4. Richard Gaffin, *Oneironautics*
5. Ryan Gattis, *The Big Drop: Impermanence*
6. Alex Sargeant, *Sci-Fidelity*
7. Veronica Bane, *Mara*
8. Kevin Staniec, *Begin*
9. Arianna Basco, *Palms Up*
10. Douglas Cowie, *Sing for Life: Tin Pan Alley*
11. Tomas Moniz, *Bellies and Buffalos*
12. Brett Arnold, *Avalon, Avalon*
13. Douglas Cowie, *Sing for Life: Away, You Rolling River*

14. Pam Jones, *The Biggest Little Bird*

15. Peppur Chambers, *Harlem's Awakening*

16. Katherine Thurmond, *Spelled*

17. Veronica Bane, *Miyuki*

18. William Brandon, *Silence*

Special Editions

1. Kevin Staniec, *29 to 31: A Book of Dreams*

Dedicated to my family Shakir, Darnell, Brooke, Kennedy, Baron, Althea, Roscoe and especially my momma, Vicki for giving me my first journal and encouraging me to do what I do: write.

Prologue.

Harlem's delicate fingers desperately reached for the smooth pearl handle of the pistol hidden under her pillow. She'd stolen it from her mother's bureau earlier that morning in the event that what was happening right now could be stopped from ever happening again.

She held the gun underneath the pillow, feeling its cool reassurance of freedom in her hand. With her head on her pillow, she laid in a trance as she turned her cheek to look at the tear-drop crystals which dangled from the chandelier lamp on her night stand. The light had not been turned on this evening. There was no need to illuminate anything. Still, in the dark, she could make out the cluster of crystals. She could hear them, better still. They clinked against one another lightly as though there were a gentle earthquake. Clink. Clink. Clink. She counted how many times one crystal kissed another as she disappeared into a fantastic ballroom where each counted clink became her first step in a *pique* turn of a romantic ballet waltz...twenty-four, twenty-five, twenty-six... She counted and twirled until the pacing of the clinks no longer matched the slow pace of the melodic, rhythmic lullaby she sang in her head for her dance.

The waltz became too fast. As it always did. The crystals were banging into one another now and she didn't want them to break. She freed her grip on the pearl handle, extended her arm from beneath the pillow and reached across to the night stand to steady the chandelier. She squeezed her eyes shut tightly. And waited.

Her bed squeaked incessantly, fervently, violently. She preferred the clink over the squeak but she hadn't much choice. And then it stopped. Harlem released the base of the lamp so she could cover her face with her arm to ward off his sweat as he fell forward and grunted in her ear. He sounded like the hogs on her granddad's farm as they hunted for fermented orange rinds. She knew the grunt all too well. He was through. And so was she. As he dismounted her like an old farm horse, he breathlessly praised her for being a good girl as he tied his pajamas.

Harlem slowly pulled herself up onto her knees. Both hands now gripped her salvation. She called his name, "Daddy..."

Even in the distorted silvery moonlight she could see the belittling amusement in his fifty-two-year-old eyes.

"Guess you ain't as good a girl as I thought," he said.

"No. I. Ain't." She pulled the trigger. His body reeled backwards and with a neck-breaking thud, he hit her pale orange sherbet bedroom wall. This room, decorated by her mother, was the proper boudoir for a young woman of her age and family standing in the community. Four-poster bed with matching night stands, lace curtains at the windows. A dressing table adorned with her toiletries, all painted a crisp white. The walls were the only color in the room which bathed it in a soft glow of dawn no matter the time of day or season. Susannah had insisted Harlem accept this color for her boudoir. Susannah never imagined how the color would look against her husband's trail of tomato-red blood.

Roy slid down the wall. Harlem pulled the trigger again. And again. And again. She felt herself shrieking but could hear nothing until her mother's voice jolted her from wherever her subconscious mind had pulled her.

"Stop it! Stop it! Stop it!" Susannah screamed. It was too late.

Susannah stood frozen in the doorway. Her chiffon night gown cascaded around her lithe figure. She looked like a beautiful bronze, soulless statue. Susannah turned on the light which revealed the beauty shared between mother and daughter and the ugly that lay dead before them.

"What have you done?" Susannah whispered.

"Momma?"

"We were working through this. He said...he said this was the last time..." The words trickled out of her like rusty water in a clogged spigot.

"I couldn't wait," Harlem said.

"Bring me the gun."

"Momma, I can't," Harlem replied. She wanted to obey her mother but her body couldn't respond because to do that Harlem would have to step over her dead father's body. And that was something she did not want to do.

"Bring it to me!" Susannah shouted. Those were the last words her mother ever said to her.

Harlem unraveled herself from her bed and sidestepped her way to her mother; her bare feet tip-toeing around Roy's lifeless body. Her mother outstretched her hand and Harlem

3

felt the softness of it as she placed the gun there. Susannah's pale grey eyes looked past Harlem into nothingness. Even in this state, her skin, the color of sandpaper, was luminous. Her hair, loosened from the braid that hung down her back, was tinged with forty-three years' worth of coarse silver strands of experience. Experiences like Harlem's breech birth eighteen years ago to unending disappointments in decisions she'd made and hadn't made resulting in days like today.

Susannah had been a fighter. She'd been a woman who could say no in several languages and with the emphatic strength of ten men. Her parents had raised her to be such and given her every opportunity to be such. It was their family way. Roy had taken her strength or maybe, over time, she'd carelessly given it. She hated being weak. Hated what it had done to her. Hated whom she'd become that day after she realized why her beautiful twelve-year-old daughter never looked her in the eye anymore or why Roy took to drinking in the middle of the day and snapped at her whenever she inquired about where he'd been. She hated because she had done nothing. That day, those seeds of hate sprouted in her quickly and spread through her veins like the disease Roy was. It ate her alive and she relished in the pain she deserved. She lived in that pain as she knew Harlem lived in hers.

As Susannah waited for the gun and stood in the home that her family built and she helped destroy, she finally felt relieved.

"Momma...?" Harlem desperately wiped Roy's warm blood from her bare foot as she watched her mother take the pistol.

Susannah walked gingerly, oddly down the hallway. The white chiffon floated as though she were a ghost in the shadows. She reached the bathroom and closed the door.

Harlem followed her. Harlem imagined she was stepping in the exact same places that her mother just had. She imagined her mother's soles had left something for her in the plush burgundy rugs that lined the highly-polished wood floors. Harlem wanted to take from those rugs what she had not been given: Warmth. Guidance. Protection. But she couldn't because it hadn't been there to give. That is why, as Harlem stood breathless outside the bathroom door, she knew that her mother stepped into her favorite porcelain bathtub, turned on her favorite silver faucet that willingly unleashed a stream of scalding hot water and drew her favorite pistol to her head and shot herself.

CHAPTER 1

Greensboro, North Carolina. 1945.

"Ms. Markeson?"

The lawyer, Mr. Thomas Hatch, Esquire, of Hatch & Hatch LTD, called her name again. He put his arms on his large gleaming mahogany desk and pushed his head forward to get her attention. Harlem had sat in front of Mr. Hatch many times over the past year and whenever he did that, he looked like a massive turtle. His bulging eyes bore into hers while his nose flared to reveal large, round nostrils. Harlem became a five-year-old caught with a forbidden sugar cookie stuffed in her mouth when he did this.

Harlem stared at him blankly. She had to because otherwise she would laugh. Her blank stare just made his nostrils flare bigger and his mouth pucker into a wrinkled beak. Harlem's hand flew to her mouth to trap the giggle that was bubbling up her throat. That urge quickly dissipated and caramelized into disdain as she rolled her eyes and thought,

"Why must I endure this?" She fidgeted in the smooth leather seat which matched his desk then turned her head to stare out his large picture window. The office was on the third floor in a statuesque building at the end of town so it got the best of the city and the county. Harlem looked past the corner drugstore across the street and out to the horizon. She could almost make out the long row of willow trees that marked the start to her family property.

She absently reached under her navy blue pencil skirt and pulled at her stockings. The clasp of the garter had been digging into her leg. She was not accustomed to wearing these things.

"Ms. Markeson!"

"Yes, yes, so sorry," she replied. Harlem removed her hand from under her skirt and clasped her hands in her lap. Even though Mr. Hatch was a nice chestnut brown, she could see the deep red flush coming up his well-educated neck and into his cheeks. This, too, was something Harlem had witnessed over the past year.

"You were saying?" Harlem said.

"You might want to pay attention, Miss. Against our advice but according to your incessant wishes, we've finally liquidated your family's assets and sold the home your grandfather built. As the sole heir to all that the Markeson family is and was, this unfortunately is your right. Further, today, you've finally been awarded your inheritance. All of this work, accomplished with my careful attention, has been done with no thanks from you, which of course, should be forthcoming to me." His face was red and scrunched into a mass of frustrated wrinkles.

"Well, how much is it?"

"A handsome sum," Mr. Hatch replied, more relaxed now that he had her attention.

"*How* handsome?" she asked.

"Very." The thin metal tip of his ink pen scratched against the grains of the fine Hatch & Hatch letterhead. She peered over the desk as Mr. Hatch reluctantly signed his name to an official-looking document. He asked Harlem to sign as well, which she did. Quickly. He blotted the ink dry while looking at her. He then, albeit reluctantly, handed her a cashier's check.

Harlem looked at the check discretely as she knew a refined woman should, but when she saw all the zeros following the number five on the check, she couldn't help from shouting, "Holy Bananas!"

Mr. Hatch cleared his throat and tried to wipe the red off his neck with his pocket kerchief. "Ms. Markeson. We've handled your family's estate now for decades…"

Harlem quickly gathered her eggshell-white leather gloves and matching navy and white hand bag. "Family's done now, in'it?"

He rose with her as Harlem made her way to the door. "That is a very large sum of money, and you should think about…"

Harlem stopped, and said very, very carefully, "I deserve every penny of it."

"You're a young woman. Only eighteen with so little outside life experience. I know you've been through a lot here in Greensboro, but perhaps…perhaps, maybe…," He stumbled. His face got redder.

"Yes?" Harlem asked.

"I would have no problem, whatsoever, even given the circumstances, to be the man who could…"

She leaned forward some. "Could what?"

"Who could…" He cleared his throat of what sounded like a thousand frogs. "Who could, could take care of you."

"Mr. Hatch! Are you trying to say what I think you're trying to say?"

"If you'd have me."

"Maybe if I'd die first!" She blurted and then corrected herself upon reaction from his stunned bulging turtle face. "I mean, that is such a *wonderful* offer but I'd probably die first here in Greensboro what with how folks here feel about me. I doubt you could take care of that, Mr. Hatch. No disrespect, of course."

Harlem paused as she walked out the door. She'd been so rude. She returned to him, removed her glove and offered her hand. "Mr. Hatch, thank you. For everything."

In spite of it all, he took her hand, warmly. It was probably the friendliest encounter they'd had over this long, long year. Harlem looked into his eyes which actually were very kind if not slightly wrinkled around the edges, and smiled. A little.

"New York is such a big city, Ms. Markeson. And…" They both paused as the clock at the Town Hall gonged twice.

"Well, in one hour I'll be on my way there!" She adjusted her gloves which were a size too big and pulled the thin netting from her chapeau back down over her eyes. "I'll be fine, I'm sure. And Mr. Hatch, my mother didn't name me 'Harlem' for nothin.' She'd want me to go."

Harlem walked by Mr. Hatch's secretary, Mildred, who had the eyes and nose of a hawk. She nodded curtly to the young woman then immediately began to type. Harlem's heels clicked against the highly buffed floor as she rushed through the office filled with rows of law clerks in their double-breasted suits. They also suddenly became very busy as she passed them. Harlem focused on the double glass doors which would lead her out of this crypt.

She pushed open the doors and with a sigh of relief walked out of the office into the bright North Carolina sun. It blinded her almost as much as the flashbulbs did going off in her face, but didn't make her nearly as angry.

"Ms. Markeson, did you get it?" reporters yelled. "Did you get the money?!"

Harlem usually ignored them but she couldn't hold it in any longer. "That is none of your damn business!"

Every time Harlem came to visit Mr. Hatch, they came with her. Every single time. And every single time they hurled the same questions at her: *"Did you get the money? Did you get the money?!"* She didn't understand why these people were so interested in her. Why was anyone interested in her?

Mr. Thomas Hatch, Esquire wanting her hand in marriage didn't truly count because he was a turtle. And what's a turtle attracted to? Bugs and worms and dried up lettuce. So the fact that he wanted her didn't exactly mean much. Plus, she'd looked at herself in the mirror, plenty of times, and what looked back at her was plain and distorted. The eyes and ears and nose and mouth were all in the right places. She wasn't hideous. Nothing near a freak of nature but what she felt like on the inside was what was seeping through to her outside. It came out of her when she cried and left a residue on her face like the ashy, dried paint on an automobile left in the sun to tarnish. It lived in her hair and made it do lackluster things. It showed up in her fingers and made her want to sit on them. The inside made her shoulders lean forward and made her head follow so that she saw more of her shoes and the ground they walked on rather than the blue sky that lived above her. The inside made her ugly.

She had been pretty once. She'd been pretty when she was eight years old, when she and her mother would practice ballet in a room of mirrors. Susannah would *jeté* and Harlem would follow. The music lifted them high in the air and landed them with ease and laughter. She'd been pretty when she was nine years old and she would sit at her mother's vanity and powder her neck with dust that smelled of new roses. She'd been pretty then, for a short while, but never reached beautiful like her mother had been back then. Yes, she was dressed in her mother's suit now but she knew she was merely a hanger, a coat rack wearing a dead woman's clothing. Harlem had yet to embody what had preceded her. She'd been trying but she had yet to succeed. She just kinda figured that she'd lost those years that lots of folks used to define themselves. Harlem had hoped they were canned up somewhere inside her like a jar of pickled peppers waiting to be enjoyed. But she feared, like old folks do, that the time had passed, never to be recovered.

The past year had been no different as Harlem spent it very, very alone. Unable to venture or spend much time in any room that Roy had, she found herself sleeping in the dance room, the room with the mirrors. She slept on a fur coat in the center of the room. She'd laid there for several days, only rising to relieve herself. George, her family's driver who'd basically become a part of their family, came by once a week with groceries she hardly ever ate and a newspaper to help her know what day it was. Harlem often threw those in the fireplace because she was usually in it.

That's why she wanted to go to New York City, where time went fast and where there were lots of people to see and do and maybe they would rub off on her and she would come alive. Maybe the face in the mirror would become undistorted and she would see her new self, the one free of Roy and free of bad things that made her walk in line with the shadows and speak with the whispers of the wind rather than with real-live folk at dinner parties and such. Maybe in New York she would be turned on.

She hurried down the sun-baked concrete steps and walked through the reporters and past a few townsfolk who had been friends of Roy's and constituents of her grandfather. These particular folks didn't care or want to know about the money. They wanted much more.

"Murderer," they yelled. "You deserve to be hanged!"

They were there to serve the justice they felt she'd evaded. Had she not stood trial, humiliated by the truth which her spirit screamed against as it was antagonized by the burning spotlight of accusations determined to define her brutal actions? Had she not sat there, virtually alone, in that court room that smelled of her mother's hope chest, naked to their stares and whispers? She didn't need these people to make her feel what they felt she deserved. It was over. She'd been proven not guilty by a jury of her peers. The jury had ruled in favor of self-defense, which it clearly was. She'd needed to defend herself against Roy's incessant need to wrong her. She'd needed to make things right – for herself and by herself since there was no one else to do so. Not her mother, not a teacher, nor a maid, a friend, the butcher, the gardener, or the man at the drugstore who used to give her ice cream. No one knew. She could tell no one. As far as the press and the good people of Greensboro Township knew, Roy had merely gotten drunk that night and attacked her. As the only surviving witness, that's what she'd told them. And that's the way it looked and smelled when the police came to get Roy and her mother that night.

People knew Roy was a drunk. That helped her. Susannah killing herself was the mystery folks couldn't understand. How could they? No one knew the real truth and that was why there was no real sympathy for her. Yet, these simple-minded folks took time out of their day to make signs to hold up to her face like a mirror to display how much they cared about her now, when no one cared about her before. But they didn't *care*. They hated. Her.

Harlem tried hard not to look anyone in the eye as she rushed to her car. She clutched her fortune close to her and did her best to focus on George who waited for her anxiously at their dark grey Ford with the door open. She was focusing so hard that she didn't see Mrs. Catrice Whitscomber until it was too late. Being of the same age and social class as Susannah, Mrs. Whitscomber was her mother's dearest friend. She was a woman who had changed Harlem's diapers and had spent countless teas at their home.

Mrs. Whitscomber had been the one to get Susannah the Benzedrine she needed to make it through the days and the strong sleeping pills to make it through her nights. Mr. Whitscomber was a doctor and was happy to dole out the pills and powders to her as he believed it hindered his wife from asking for other things.

The two women had been working to create the Markeson Dance Academy. This had been Mrs. Whitscomber's idea because she believed that if Susannah could get back to dancing, the thing she loved the most, that she'd be fine. That the assured boredom haunting her would dissipate and she could laugh with her dear friend again. They'd actually met privately with bankers the day Susannah died. Now, Mrs. Whitscomber blamed Harlem for everything. For the past year, Mrs. Whitscomber had mourned, but more than that, she'd spent nights scrutinizing, dissecting and questioning the fact that although Roy had not been the best husband, Susannah *must* have cared for him much more than she'd ever let on during any of their conversations. Why else would she act so? She surmised that Harlem killing Roy undoubtedly sent Susannah utterly and desperately over the edge. Mrs. Whitscomber thought Harlem was selfish, foolish, and greedy. An ungrateful bitch for ending two lives, one of which she loved as much as any friend could.

Harlem saw Mrs. Whitscomber's pale brown eyes swimming with rage. Harlem assumed what she saw was an extension of her own feelings. Harlem reached for her, expecting a hug from this woman who had loved Harlem as her own daughter. Instead, Mrs. Whitscomber raised her meaty hand and slapped Harlem square across her sallow cheek.

"Shame on you!" she spat. And then she spit at Harlem's new pair of white traveling shoes.

In the beginning, Roy would slap Harlem to get her to stop crying. She learned very early on to stop crying when Roy got started with her. Still, he'd never slapped her as hard as Mrs. Whitscomber just had. Harlem staggered from the force of the blow and stood bewildered as the crowd formed a circle around her. Mrs. Whitscomber had disappeared, apparently satisfied with her lick. Harlem could see the others wanted the same opportunity. She supposed they'd been waiting a good long time for this moment. After both funerals and after the months she spent in the Lofton Reform School for Girls waiting for her trial, along with the months she spent as a recluse in the eerie, empty home waiting for today, they were good and ready. Shit, so was she! The difference was that she was waiting for her life to begin and they wanted hers to end. These people saw her as a child who had killed her father and drove her mother to suicide. All for money. They were dead wrong.

She felt someone grab her arm. Panicked, she began to fight off whomever was bold enough to take the first move to make this mob grow like a tick engorged with blood after a good feeding. She looked at her captor and saw it was George who had her. George was in his seventies but he was strong.

"Get back," he shouted as he shoved the pack of fools aside. Some of them were his friends. "Ya'll should be 'shamed of y'selves treatin' this girl this way. Was an accident! Accidents happen ev'ry day in this world. Get back!"

Harlem clung to George as he led her to the safety of the car. Like a dog herded into a kennel, she jumped in. She landed on the cream leather seat clumsily and banged her wrist on the waiting Samsonite suitcase with its Bakelite handle.

"Ouch," Harlem cried. And then she really cried.

George settled into the driver's seat and got them out of there.

Harlem fought with the dark blue dotted netting from her veiled hat as she tried to catch her tears in her handkerchief. She leaned her head back on the seat and wailed.

"I didn't do anything!"

"You alright, Miss?" George knew she wasn't. He wasn't either. As bad a drunk as Roy had been, Roy was still his friend and his employer, and he missed him terribly. He and Roy used to go pheasant hunting. Sometimes they'd be out there for hours traipsing through the tall brush on the acres of the Markeson property like they were school boys. They'd bring a lunch, and of course Roy would bring an old jug of his rum, and they'd hunt. Sometimes they'd talk and sometimes they wouldn't. Even in silence a man can get to know another man. Lots of times, Roy would start to talk and would just start crying.

George knew Roy had run away from his father's Ohio farm at an early age and got himself to New York. The way Roy described it, his father had been a tyrant of a man, but back then whose daddy had time to be nice? George barely remembered his own father. Remembered him leaving early in the morning for work on a tobacco farm and returning late in the evening to the arms of his mother who would wash and bandage his raw hands. George knew it was hard for a man to be a man. Over the years, he gathered something had happened to Roy when he was young that messed with his core real good. George never got to know what that was. But he did know that when Roy met Susannah, and Susannah's family money, it came right on time for filling the hole in his being that he alone did not have the power or no longer had the wherewithal to do. Susannah became his glue. Then he started to resent her for it. George often wondered how people ask for something and then when they get it, they want to be mad at it for coming.

"Miss, I want you t' know that I'm going to miss you somethin' awful," he said. "Understand?"

Harlem covered her face and nodded.

"And, even though ain't no more physical home to call home, that this place is your home and I s'pose I'm kinda your only family now, if'n you ever wanted to b'lieve I was your family...."

"I know, George," she whispered.

"So, number one, when you get over there to New York, you be careful. I ain't never been there, but your fath—well, I heard that place can be some kinda wonderful. And I want you t' enjoy ev'ry moment of it and t' find the happ'ness you been missin' in your life. You hear me?"

She nodded.

"And number two. I can't make you reach out t' me or write me or let me know how you're farin' but, should you decide that that is somethin' you might want or need to do, then I am goin' to be open to it. I will be most welcomin' of it."

George wiped sorrow away from his own cheek, which even after seventy-two years, was smooth like satin and kept the color of the dried tobacco his father harvested. George had never married nor had children of his own, except for Harlem. And though she'd been a child who always seemed a million miles away, he would miss her. He pulled up to the bus depot.

"Y' ready, Miss?"

Harlem tried her best to compose herself. She wanted to leave so very badly, but somehow she felt glued to her seat. She sat looking out the window of the car.

"Miss Harlem. I been knowing you your whole entire life. You ain't never been one to speak a whole lot, but I hear you right now." George got himself out of the Ford and opened the door for Harlem. He took her by the wrist and pulled her out gently. He then walked slowly around to the trunk to get the rest of her suitcases and let her be.

"George," Harlem called after a while.

He brought the monogrammed dark brown, marbleized luggage that he'd carried many times for Mrs. Markeson, to her feet. "Yes'm?"

"Thank you."

He reached into his black driving coat and pulled her bus tickets from his pocket. He handed them to her. "You're welcome, Miss Harlem."

She hugged him long and hard, which he knew to mean, *"I love you, George."* She didn't have to say it for him to know it. He knew she didn't know how to say it. He hoped one day she would learn how. George hugged her back as hard as he could to let her know he felt the same. Then, he got into the car and drove away. He wanted to turn back and look at Harlem one last time, but it was better for both of them if he didn't.

CHAPTER 2

The Greensboro bus depot was nothing more than a shack with a long platform. It was trying to become something more, but it was not there yet. Kind of like Harlem. It smelled of rotting wood, fresh paint, and cigarettes and it reminded Harlem of when her mother used to take her on weekends to ride horses at Drisden Stables. The stables had belonged to her grandparents. They'd sold it when she was about five, but the family that bought it still let them ride whenever they wanted. She'd enjoyed that time alone with her mother, and she loved the freedom she felt when she galloped through the wild-flower fields on Lulu, a muddy-brown mare. She stopped going to the stables all together around when she was fourteen after Roy took her instead and tried to put his hand on her ass as she mounted. Roy always had a way of ruining things.

Rows of women and men, waiting so close together, looked like the paper dolls she had cut out as a child from the brown paper sacks kept in the kitchen. Women in their

Sunday best, men in shirts with jackets draped over their shoulders, men in uniform, and families with crying children stood as shining specs of dust swirled about them in the sunlight. Were they too looking for the wind to fill them with something other than the life they were currently living? Harlem thought this as she stepped into a sliver of shade and stood perfectly still like a life-sized kite waiting for her own gust.

Sweat trickled in places a lady shouldn't sweat, made her slip stick to the curve of her back. She hated that feeling and quickly pulled the silk from her skin. The shift allowed two more ambitious drops to slide from her collar bone and down between her Matildas. When she was just about twelve, they'd gone to visit Roy's family the one and only time. His mother, her grandma, had turned from the bacon she was frying up and said, "Honey, I see your Matildas is startin' to bud. That means the boys is gon' come 'round tryin' to hoe down a pretty gal like you. You gotta learn to protect what's yours so's you don't seem too available n' easy. Better get you a big stick so's you'll be ready to beat 'em down." Grandma Markeson turned out to be right, just like grandma's usually are. Only, the "boy" that started comin' round wasn't a boy at all.

She looked down as someone passed. It had become a habit. Harlem focused on her shoes. It made her look busy. Dust covered them, except in the spots where Mrs. Whitscomber had spit on them. The spit spots were like daggers jabbing at her insides. It hurt to look at them. It was all she could do to stop herself from rubbing them on the back of her stockings in order to forget. Instead she took her damp handkerchief from her pocket book and wiped away at the hurt. She rubbed at the white leather on her T-strap pumps until they shone.

Harlem walked to a trash basket and dropped the soiled handkerchief into the receptacle, hoping she could throw the memory away along with it. Who was she fooling? So, as she was prone to do during times like this, Harlem went deep inside herself, just to the left and behind her heart, and found her peace keeper. It was a wooden box, shaped almost like a tiny coffin and that's where she put this memory of Mrs. Whitscomber spitting on her. The box was full of recollections such as this, so she hurriedly closed the box, lest one decided to jump out and strangle her. She had to get rid of that coffin box somehow. Simply forget everything. Certainly she didn't want surgery or anything quite as drastic as what medical quacks did to women when no one was watching, but she sure had something that needed to be cut out. Sometimes, when she got too comfortable, that coffin box would open on its very own and the stuff inside would wiggle out and worm down into her stomach and then crawl back up through her spine and wrap itself around her head and squeeze out any rational or peaceful thinking she had left. She made sure the coffin box was shut tight. She then left her inside and returned to where she'd been standing.

Everything was how she'd left it: still hot and still dusty. Harlem realized she was still looking down at her spotless shoes, so she lifted her head, thereby pulling her shoulders back and forcing her chin out, ready to face the world square on.

She wasn't sure how long she'd been on her inside. She looked up at the large round clock hanging just under the station's sign. The clock's black, metal arms pointed like arrows at the eleven and the three. Luckily, she'd only been gone ten minutes or so, this time. Sometimes she could disappear for up to thirty minutes at a time. Looking at the clock now, she got excited. And nervous. Bus was due to arrive at 3:15.

Her chin started to hurt, especially on the left side where Mrs. Whitscomber had slapped her, so she had to stop facing the world for a moment. She opened her smaller Samsonite train case and found another handkerchief to replace the one she'd been forced to throw away. She loved all of her handkerchiefs. She'd embroidered some herself; others had been given to her over the years for birthdays and a few she'd taken from her mother's collection. The one she held now was from that collection. It was of the finest cotton, and its edges were stitched with the palest pink. The corners were dotted with yellow and green flowers. In the center were her mother's initials, "SM," stitched in azure blue, her mother's trademark.

"Miss?"

Startled, Harlem turned to the man. "What?"

He flinched as her fiery eyes heavily investigated him. "Pardon me. Just wondered if you'd like t' sit?" he mustered.

"Thank you. No."

"Fine by me." He snapped the pages of his GREENSBORO TIMES, flicking the newspaper open. The front page faced her with its stinging headline, hurting as much as Mrs. Whitscomber's slap: ONE YEAR LATER, MARKESON MURDER/SUICIDE STILL SHOCKS TOWN!

Harlem froze as she stared at the face that was supposed to be her own plastered underneath the glaring headline. She thought nothing matched except the eyes drawing her back to the coffin box. She felt her pin curl drop again on her eyelid.

She adjusted it as quickly as it had been dislodged on the front steps of the Hatch & Hatch offices

He peeked at her from around his paper. He noticed her proud, lean legs as she balanced on her white high heels like a ballerina. Her hourglass frame was petite and he imagined he could fit the hatband of his chocolate brown Fedora around her waist. Her navy suit, sophisticated. Even without learning so from the paper, he could tell she came from money. He was surprised by his own curiosity of her. He watched her slow breathing as she pressed her handkerchief to her breast. Her brown skin glistened like the warm, buttered toast he had eaten for breakfast. He deciphered that her quiet demeanor could speak the language of beauty when it was allowed to speak. It was the gaze from her velvet amber eyes that had caused him to flinch. He'd caught her off-guard, it seemed. She revealed in the flash of her eyelash a wave of fury that could drown any man.

Still curious, he ventured out into her water and sent a gentle *tsk' tsk* as he said, "Too bad about that girl."

Harlem knew without looking that he was talking about her. Looking at her. She hurriedly fanned herself unsuccessfully with her gloved hand. In her haste, she turned her pocket book topsy-turvy and its contents fluttered out.

The man rose to help her but it was the big-boned woman who had been sitting next to him who moved like a flash of lightening to help Harlem. He'd never seen a woman her size move so quickly.

"Here you are, Miss," the woman cooed as she gently offered Harlem her compact and coin purse. Harlem gathered her ticket and other loose items.

"My lipstick! Where's it gone?"

The man searched for Harlem's lipstick that had rolled underneath the wooden bench where he and the ample woman had been sitting.

"Here it is, Miss," The man handed her the lipstick and returned to his seat.

Harlem blushed a thousand shades of red as she watched her things being man-handled by strangers. "Thank you," she sighed.

The man watched as the big-boned woman still held onto an envelope which had fallen from Harlem's purse.

"Hatch & Hatch Limited," she read aloud. She then turned toward another woman who was just coming from the restroom off to the left of the depot.

"Sister, look at this," she said as she waved the envelope like a dishrag. "Hatch & Hatch. Isn't this the law outfit where you were formerly employed?"

He observed as Harlem tried to politely retrieve her envelope like a child getting her ball back from bullies on a playground.

The thinner sister of the two took the envelope. "Why yes, yes it was. What a coincidence." They both turned and looked at Harlem inquisitively.

Harlem stared blankly back at them.

The man watched and even though both sisters smiled he knew he was looking at a pair of shifty vultures.

"Won't you forgive us," the larger one remarked. "My name is Sister Ruth, and this here is Sister Mary."

"Hello. How do you do?" Harlem's attention diverted to the grumbling arrival of her future as it pulled into the depot.

The man quickly grabbed the envelope and returned it to Harlem. "Life is full of coincidences. But I think that bus is much more interestin' right now."

Harlem stuffed the envelope back in her handbag, "I'd have to agree. Thank you," she said as she studied the accountant-type man. He seemed near his fifties if not in them and he had an outward enthusiasm that did not fully match his pallid cheeks and sad brown eyes. She picked up her suitcases in anticipation of the bus.

The sisters hurried for their own things as they called out, "Was a pleasure to meet you!"

Harlem nodded politely in their direction as the man said, "Lemme help y' with that suitcase, Miss Pretty."

Harlem had had enough with strangers touching her things. "I'm quite fine, thank you," she bristled.

The man smiled gallantly. "Well, that we can see. But that isn't necessr'ly the point at hand. But since I'm speakin' of hands, let me offer mine."

"I don't need any help, sir."

"Well, I was actually talkin' about me reachin' my right hand out to yours like so," he said as he gently took hers even though it was hooked around a suitcase. "And then we'd get to know one another for this here long trip to the New York City." He continued to hold her hand, hoping he could withstand the furious tidal wave swelling in her eyes.

"See here? Now this is the part where I say, 'Good Aft'noon. My name is Mr. Jonas Stewart' and you say, 'Good Aft'noon Mr. Stewart. My name is...' And then you fill in the blank."

Harlem stared at him. "I fill in the blank?"

"Yes, Miss. You fill in the blank unless'n you want me to call you Miss Pretty all the way to the New York City."

Harlem hadn't wanted him to call her anything, let alone her real name. Harlem Winnepega Markeson was a name that always encouraged unnecessary conversation, especially lately. And like right now. He also hadn't let go of her hand which made her want to punch him in the nose for being nosy and for not getting the hint that she'd wanted to be left alone. She remained a lady and conjured a semblance of a smile to use.

"Alright then, Mr. Jonas Stewart, since you are so persistent, my name is Miss Smith. Ann Smith."

"Would that be with an 'E' or without?"

"Sorry?"

"Ann. 'E' or No 'E'?"

Harlem could hardly stand it. "No 'E'. Thank you." She quickly pulled her hand from his. Only, since her mother's glove was a size too big, it stayed with Mr. Stewart instead of with her.

He smothered a chuckle as he returned the item. He noticed the supple, leather glove was monogrammed with "S.M."

"Interesting thing here Miss Ann, if that S here on your gloves is for 'Smith,' what then is the M for?"

Harlem slapped the gloves impatiently against her thigh. "The 'S' is for Susannah. These belonged to my mother; Susannah." The bus sighed to a gravelly stop. Weary passengers exited. As bad as they looked, Harlem was eager to take one of their vacant seats.

Jonas looked down at her suitcase. "Suitcases got the SM too, I see. Well, your mother has very nice tastes."

She twisted to see a seat on the bus through the windows. "Yes, she did." Harlem picked up her cases and ran for the line which was now twice as long as it had been.

"Sure is nice to meet you, Miss Smith," Jonas called after her.

Harlem gawked at the NEW YORK CITY destination sign that beckoned from the side of the bus. She was awestruck as she shuffled into line, jostled by the crowd. She surveyed her fellow travelers: She was like no one else and no one else was like her. Harlem was also the only woman traveling alone. She hadn't thought about securing a chaperone. Who was there for her to ask, anyway? Certainly not Mrs. Whitscomber. Not Mr. Hatch. Not even George, whom just now at the mere thought of him, summoned a sting in the back of her throat that wanted to pull a trigger on her tears again. She clamped her eyes shut and held her breath to halt the impending torrential downpour. She couldn't have an episode like she'd had in the car. Certainly not in front of all these strangers. Even though she knew George was long gone and she was relieved to be ditching Greensboro, she turned to take a final look back at what she was leaving behind. She inadvertently made eye contact with the sisters who had just cut in line in front of Mr. Stewart and swiftly fallen into step directly behind Harlem.

They quickly looked away, leaving Mr. Stewart in full view. He tipped his fedora at Harlem. As soon as she turned, he tugged his hat low over his eyes as he observed Ruth and Mary watching Harlem.

CHAPTER 3

Harlem stood before a sea of faces: brown, black, caramel, and cream. Most stared at her. She didn't belong. She couldn't have been more inspected if she'd been a three-headed tadpole. Harlem pulled her perfumed lace handkerchief from her brassier and dabbed at her throat. She felt their eyes measure her up. Taking notes. Inspecting her layer by layer and recording their findings as she passed them by.

Harlem walked toward the back of the bus and spotted an open window seat next to a young mother.

"Mind I sit at the window?" Harlem asked politely. Harlem thought she looked too young to be tending to the child seated across the aisle from her who was happily swinging his legs from his seat. The mother agreed to the seating arrangement. Harlem slid into her safe seat to find Jonas coming down the aisle. Somehow, he'd gotten his positioning back and was in front of the sisters, who now trailed a few paces behind him.

He, too, asked the young mother if he could sit by the window. He pointed to the opposite window seat which was next to her child, who seemed about five. The little boy sized up Jonas, looked at his mother, and smiled brightly.

"That'd be fine," the mother replied.

Jonas shook the young man's hand as he settled into the seat. The boy giggled and seemed quite happy to have Jonas as his new companion.

Sister Ruth and Sister Mary jostled down the aisle toward them with Ruth's large frame hiding most of her sister. Harlem thought they would knock each other over if they went any faster. Ruth's skin was like smooth caramel. Her full lips pursed and brown eyes sparkled as Harlem examined Ruth's face more closely. Her green dress swayed about her round calves. Ruth's broad curves skimmed past row after row of travelers. Mary's bright complexion was just as smooth as her sister's. Her thin lips offset her wide eyes while her collar bones poked through her white blouse, cradling a long neck crowned by an authoritative chin. Harlem turned her head to the window as her thoughts saddened. Her mother would have been about their age.

"I hope you don't take us to be rude, dear. But would you mind if my sister and I take your seat and your child's?" Ruth inquired.

The sisters had backed up and were now grinning greedily at seats already occupied.

"You see, we make this trip to New York City once a year and we always try to sit the number of rows back that we've been making the trip," Mary added. "This year makes twelve."

"Twelve years makes twelve rows," chimed Ruth. "Next year we'd sit in row thirteen."

"Thirteen? I doubt I'll be sittin' in any row thirteen for fifteen hours, Sister Ruth. Thirteen is not a good number."

"That's neither here nor there, Sister Mary."

The few remaining unseated passengers attempted to squeeze past the sister's imposed blockade, pressing the sisters even closer upon the helpless mother and child wedged between them.

"Well, it 'tis, just not at this moment, per se," Mary said.

"Let's not argue Mary," Ruth smiled. People now turned around and started to whisper about what was happening behind them. Most were agitated and the trip hadn't even begun.

"I'm not arguing, Ruth," Mary insisted, raising her voice.

"But you *are*, Mary," Ruth said, even louder.

From the front, the driver bellowed, "Find your seats! Find your seats!"

The mother was becoming embarrassed as folks now began looking at her to do something,. "You can have our seats," the mother whispered, dragging her son who began to wail in protest with her as she rose and claimed the empty seats behind them.

"Why thank you, dear," Ruth said. "You're so kind. And you understand we wouldn't ask you except that…"

"Twelve years," Mary concluded.

Jonas rose. "Pardon me, fine ladies. My father wouldn't let me keep his last name, Stewart, that is, if I didn't introduce myself proper and offer my seat. I am Jonas Stewart." He offered his hand to Mary. She shook the tips of his long fingers and then wiped her hand on her thigh. She looked as though she'd eaten a bowl of rotten Brussels sprouts.

"Now, let's just switcheroo an' you sisters can both sit right next to each other."

Harlem raised her eyebrows. She couldn't endure this man, as nice as he truly seemed, for such a very long trip.

"No," Ruth said as she plopped next to Harlem with such force the hem of her dress flew up over her knees revealing her modest slip.

"We both require aisle seats, sir," Mary bargained, much sweeter. "It's the gout. We've both been attacked."

Ruth nodded sternly. "Gout."

"Gout? That ain't contagious now, is it?" Jonas questioned.

Ruth laughed and elbowed Harlem in the ribs, "I don't s'pose he'd like to find out!"

Jonas eased back into his seat next to Mary and replied, "No. No, I would not. Thank you."

Ruth nodded sharply, "You see? Didn't think he wanted to find out." Ruth extended her hand, "Hello, dear."

"Hello," Harlem noticed the cuff on her shirt was tattered as she shook Ruth's hand in return and smiled.

"I never did catch your name."

"Ann Smith," Harlem lied.

"Are you related to...?"

"No."

From the corner of her eye, Harlem saw Jonas fanning himself with the newspaper and its painful headline. He spoke loud enough for Harlem to hear. "Shame about this here Markeson family, ain't it? Father dead. Mother dead. All that money, too."

Mary read her own newspaper. "Money can't buy decency. I've heard terrible things about..."

"It can buy you a fortress," Ruth interjected, with her eyes closed. "And that's what they had up there in that house. Wouldn't you agree, Ann?"

Harlem turned to the window. "I wouldn't know."

Still with her eyes closed, Ruth bellowed, "Word is, the daughter is the sole heir to the family fortune."

"Now that there is a whole 'lotta words!" Jonas joked.

Ruth opened her eyes and looked at Harlem on the sly. "Miss Smith, aren't you at all familiar with this story of murder and mayhem?"

"Isn't everyone?" Harlem answered.

"Shoot, I'm just passin' through and I feel I know quite a bit. Paper says here it all happened a year ago today," said Jonas.

"You seem to favor the girl, Ann. Isn't that an unfortunate thing to look like a murderer?"

Harlem felt the snake slithering up her spine. She was now leaning so close to the window, her breath fogged the pane. She was starting to slip to her inside.

"Sister Mary, it's not anywhere near polite to insinuate that someone looks like a *murderer*."

"I'm sure it's worse to be one." Jonas looked squarely at Mary. He was certain he saw her flinch. Harlem suddenly shot up from her seat and started gathering her things abruptly.

"Excuse me, Sister Ruth, I just don't think I can make this trip today," Harlem said.

Sister Ruth blocked her clumsily. "Well…Are you feeling alright dear? If you hurry maybe you can…"

Ruth tried to lift herself from the chair. Once this was accomplished, she dropped the book on the floor that had been resting on her lap. She bent over to pick it up. Harlem was overcome by Ruth's backside.

"Sister Ruth, if you'd just move your behind, I could…"

Mary rose and stood in front of Ruth, coaxing her out, but really was just one hundred percent in the way. Mary quipped, "I do believe the bus'll be leavin—"

And at the moment, the bus grumbled to life. The driver yelled out their destination, *"NEW YORK CITY!"* and requested everyone be sure they were on the right bus goin' to the right place.

"Driver! I'd like to get off the bus, please!" Harlem shouted.

It was then that Mary, still standing in the aisle, began to sing loudly. Her voice as shrill as a neglected tea pot. She demanded a chorus of all, *"Amazin' Grace…"*

Ruth joined in. She lifted her generous arms and they were a pair of choir directors, *"How sweet the sound…"*

Even Jonas participated, *"That saved a wretch like me…."*

Soon the young mother, her son, and the anonymous heathens and the saved joined in, including the driver who, through no fault of his own, never heard Harlem's demands. He steered the caravan off toward New York on schedule and as planned.

Harlem slumped in her seat. "Shit."

CHAPTER 4

Jonas wound his worn leather watch and placed it to his ear to make sure it was still ticking. The time piece had never failed him and he didn't expect it to start doing so now. Its square face read 6:30 p.m. and by the looks of the sun beginning its decent into the horizon, he felt it to be true. He looked over at Harlem. She had calmed herself down about two hours ago and managed to fall soundly asleep. He assumed this was something she hadn't been able to do in a long time.

Jonas quietly wrote in his journal. Since his quest began, his journal had become his companion and confidant, keeping both his secrets and his sanity. He was building a history; documenting the times, places and happenings of his life over the past three painful years. The words, sometimes, like a cup of warm bourbon and honey, soothed his aching soul. At others, they magnified the trouble that had set this quest in motion. Of course, the trouble began more than three years ago, but his pain began on July 10, 1941.

He was only fifty-three-years old. Not enough gray hairs to notice as silver. His knuckles were getting harder to bend but still nimble. He caressed them now as he blew the ink dry on the last of the five pages he'd just written. He returned his journal to his attaché and pulled his friend, his silver flask, from his suit pocket. Jonas relished its weight; it was full and that was a very good thing. He turned it round and round in his hand like a well-worn deck of cards. He'd done this so many times over the years that the engraved "J" on his flask was nearly worn smooth. The flask had been a gift from his wife on their fifth wedding anniversary. Through fifteen years of marriage, he'd had this thoughtful gift and used it often and not because his wife drove him to drink, but because he really liked the taste of whiskey and liked how he felt when he drank it even better. He loved his wife, loved her more than what he knew what to do with himself, and that's why, when she died in his arms, he was never himself again.

They'd been at home, in Kentucky. It was a summer day. Nothing they hadn't been used to or seen in their lives before. A peaceful day. He'd been fixing a loose board on the porch steps and she'd been clipping some daisies from the garden. Their daughter, 'Netta, who'd been fourteen at the time, sat on the porch swing reading a book. The sun had been beating on his forehead; he'd just grabbed the 'kerchief from his back pocket and was wiping away the toils of his labor from his brow when he heard Julia scream. He'd been just outside Julia's door when his daughter had been born; he'd heard Julia scream then. This scream wasn't like that. He'd heard her scream in fright from having a spider land on her arm. This scream wasn't like that neither. This was terror. He'd jumped up as she rushed toward him. He could see in her eyes she was wanting him to save her but he had no idea how. Her face was starting to swell. Her tongue seemed so big, that it didn't have room to stay in her mouth. Her eyes started bulging from out her head like cows did when branded. He screamed for his daughter to run to the neighbors and get help as he ran to his Julia, but he knew that would do no good. He held her by her arms, and he felt the welt where she'd been stung. That was how they'd both found out she was allergic to bee stings.

When Jonas laid his wife in the ground, he remembered how his grandmother wailed at his granddad's funeral. How his grandmother wailed and wailed and kept repeating, *"Put me in there with him! Put me in there with him!"* Back then, along with his father, he'd been the one to hold up his grandmother, 'cause the grief had taken her legs, and her heart didn't want her to do nothing but lie on the ground. Now it was his turn, but he had no one to hold him up. He'd been there for his daughter as best he could, but he knew he really wasn't because inside he was screaming, *"Put me in there with her!"*

A year after Julia's death, nothing had gotten better. Everything had gotten incredibly worse. He just hadn't been able to get the grief out of his body or his mind quick enough. And, by the time he was able, it was too late. The damage had been done. His daughter had actually been there for him and he hadn't paid attention. How many times had he sat on the porch and told her he wasn't hungry after she'd cooked for them both? How many Sundays had she gone to church alone because he couldn't speak to God any longer? There were countless times when she'd look at him like his daughter, and he looked back at her like a stranger.

Then one day she said she'd had enough and was going to the store. But she never came back. Being a strong-willed girl with pain in her heart and gumption in her spirit, she simply left. He didn't really blame her, but she was so young. And she was a girl. His baby girl. He could almost see a son leaving his home young like that and living on a farm or being able to take care of himself, but not a girl and definitely not his own daughter whom he sincerely loved with all his might. He needed her back. Wanted her back. He wrote of this every day in his journal and would do so until he found her. Would have been okay if he'd heard from her at least once in all this time, but he hadn't and that let him know something was wrong. Call it father's intuition or whatever folks may call it, but he started to get a feeling that something was wrong with his girl. That's when he started searching and asking questions about her whereabouts. The more he learned, the more he was rightfully convicted that his girl was missing. That's why when he saw a young woman like Harlem, he made sure he looked real close to make sure he wasn't looking into the eyes of his lost child. He'd seen many girls like this over the years of his search. He felt he wouldn't be looking much longer, however, because he'd gotten the best tip last month which lead him to exactly where he was right now.

He screwed the cap off his flask and the slight grinding of metal-on-metal was enough to wake up Mary. The way she fluttered her eyes open and licked her lips told him she was used to the sound, just like a dog knows the sound of a church key, whether it was being used to open his food or your own. He took a sip. Mary looked at him shyly. He thought she may have even batted an eyelash. She straightened up and got back to the needlepoint resting on her lap. Jonas looked at her work. "Everyone can't be good at everything," he thought. She smiled at him briefly but longingly as she stitched her colorful monstrosity.

Jonas grinned back as he took another sip. He thought about his next move as he listened to the chatter of the folks on the bus. Friendships had been made. Some played cards. Some sang quietly with a guitar in the back. A soldier told his war stories to a group of keen listeners, including the little boy. Jonas was ready. He put the flask back in his pocket.

Mary cleared her throat. "Dry in here, in'it?" she grinned.

Jonas radiated with kindness as he retrieved his gem and presented the flask like a silver Chalice. "Either of you fine gentle-ladies care for a sip of my secret potion?"

Mary stopped mid-stitch of her needlepoint. "Secret potion?"

Without breaking her stride, Ruth, who'd been reading her book, said no.

Jonas turned and buttered Mary like a warm biscuit, though he didn't have much buttering to do. "Whiskey doctored up in fine order, if I do say so myself."

"I said, *no.*" Ruth repeated.

"If I didn't know any better, Sister Ruth, I'd say you don't like me."

"We barely know you," Ruth, still reading, answered.

"My point exac'ly!" Jonas scoffed. "I'm tryin' to get to know you, and you would be tryin' to get to know me. 'Specially as Sisters of the Cloth. Isn't it your Godly duty to be Godly to thy Godly neighbor?"

"No."

"Ruth!" Mary scolded. She turned sweetly to Jonas. "We aren't *those* types of sisters, Mr. Stewart. Merely sisters by blood, and in this moment, I'd be happy to sever my ties. It's unfortunate if my sister seems rude, Mr. Stewart." Mary eyed the flask and again licked her lips. "But, you can understand how cautious two women traveling alone would need to be."

Jonas raised the flask so as to make eye contact with Mary. "That I can understand. I do hope you can see I mean you no harm. I'm gentle as a little fly." He twisted off the cap.

"I don't like flies," Ruth said.

"Sister Ruth, I like your honesty!" Jonas bantered, pouring a drop into the cap top which doubled as a shot glass. He elevated the shot for Mary to get a whiff of the potion's gentle, intoxicating aroma.

"I don't mind 'em, except when they're botherin' me," Mary said.

Jonas leaned into her. "Am I bothering you?"

Mary held the shot and covered it with her needlepoint. She giggled. "No, no you are not!" She lifted the shot to her grateful mouth and from behind the shield of her needlepoint, sent the doctored whiskey down the hatch.

Jonas accepted the empty cap from her and filled it again. "I see now we must have at least one thing in common, Miss Mary."

Mary, laughing, took the second shot from Jonas before he barely had a chance to finish filling it up. "That we do!" Again, the needlepoint provided her the privacy she clearly was accustomed to having when she enjoyed her libations.

"What else might there be?" Jonas suggested.

"Oh, I'm sure I wouldn't know, Mr. Stewart." He now saw her freckles. They were jumping in the red warmth flaming across her cheeks. His potion was working.

"Where're you and your sister from? Greensboro?"

"Yes. Me and Sister Ruth. Both of us. Born and raised." She paused, as if what she had to say next would bear some significance on their current situation. "She's older, you know."

Jonas filled the cap, but this one was for himself. "Now ain't that fine."

"And you, Mr. Stewart?"

He remembered to use his southern accent, his disguise, "Oh, I'm from all over. Don't exac'ly have a home no more. I travel for work. That's why I'm goin' to the New York City. Now, why are you goin' to New York?" He took a long draw on the flask.

Mary nearly fell out her seat with excitement as she watched him take in the caramel treat. "Oh. Now that's a long story."

Jonas kept the cap in his hand and offered her the entire flask. "Got plenty of time. 'Least seven or more hours!"

From across the aisle, Ruth leaned forward and placed her hands on her ham hock hips. "Sister Mary."

"Sister?" Mary, wide eyed, responded.

"My right leg is starting to cause me some pain. I might like to switch seats with you."

Mary stole another sip before answering. "Sister, why don't you just get up and walk a few steps?" She took a long drag from the flask.

Jonas wasn't sure why she still held up her needlepoint. He gently took the concoction from her as he stood. He bowed ever so slightly to Ruth. "Sister Ruth, am I no longer a fly you don't like? 'Cause I'd sure be honored to have you sit next to me."

"Never mind."

Mary giggled as Jonas sat back in his chair and she sunk deeply into hers. "She can be such a prude sometimes," she whispered. "All these years we been goin' back and forth to

New York and she still act like it's a big deal to talk to strangers!"

"She's tryin' to protect you, I'm sure," Jonas whispered back.

Still whispering, Mary scrunched her nose. "Too much, if you ask me. I'm a big girl now!"

"I can see that, Miss Mary. You've grown into quite a fine woman. How many years you been goin' back and forth to New York?"

"Twelve!" Mary, answered, ashamed.

"Twelve! That's something."

"Been making these trips for too long. I think I'm just about tired of it," she lamented.

"Always from Greensboro?"

They were huddled in their seats like children hiding under the blankets.

"Well, mostly. We have to stop along the way in other cities sometimes if we don't find what we need but we always end up in New York an' we always find what we need."

Jonas held onto his masked grin of southern hospitality as hard as he could. He felt like he was doing a tango with the devil on a tight rope. He had to keep his cool or he'd lose everything he'd worked for up 'til this very moment and he was downright terrified he was carrying a garish grimace across his face. Not wanting to frighten her, or worse, have her stop talking, he quickly offered up his whiskey.

"And what's that?" he asked. "What's that that you *need*?"

Mary swallowed three times before she lowered the flask from her lips.

"Fiiiiine goods!"

Just then, Harlem screamed some kind of bloody murder.

CHAPTER 5

Harlem felt the terror creeping into her throat but she couldn't wake fast enough to stop her dream. Roy was after her, again:

Roy grunts violently as he enters her room, steeped in shadows. He's drunk and slurs grossly at her.

"Gal. I told ya' once if not a mill'n times before, I'm gonna put you out in m' barn with the horses an' the pigs where y' belong."

Cowering from a corner of her bed, Harlem's heavy, spiteful breathing is the only answer. Roy tells her to get up but she can't move. She cringes against the wall hoping to disappear. He shouts what he always shouts. "I said get up! Alla these years of teachin' y' borin' ass to obey has juss 'bout wore me out. I feel sorry for m'self!"

He lunges toward her, but she springs from the bed while screaming in fear. In the darkness, she tumbles into her heavy dresser. Her hairbrush and pins scatter to the floor. "You wanna keep screamin' like an aminal, I'mma treat you like an aminal." He pulls his belt from his pants and whips her bare shoulder exposed from her skewed, thin nightgown. He swings quickly again and again. Catches her back and her calves. She yelps with each contact and quickly dives behind her rickety chair for cover, whimpering. She can hardly catch her breath. Her brown eyes are wide with fear and steady resentment.

Roy throws the chair aside. "You think you can get away from me like your moth'r did? Yoooouuuu ain't that smaaaarrt," he growls. He then pulls out his gun from his holster on his back, aims at her square in the eye, and pulls!

She woke explosively. Screams of the bus passengers now mingled with her own as the bus lurched and swerved dangerously on the narrow dirt road. Harlem wasn't sure what was going on until someone yelled out, "We blew a tire! Ev'rybody hold on!"

Harlem wasn't holding on to nothing and she felt herself being thrown against the window. She hollered in pain as her head smashed against the pane. Mary tumbled into the aisle while Ruth braced herself with one leg jammed against the seat in front of her.

The driver struggled with the steering wheel, and finally the roller coaster came to a terrible screeching halt.

Dripping with perspiration, the driver turned, irate. "Who the hell hollered?" His jowls jiggled like a jumpy bull dog. Everyone looked at Harlem as they collected themselves.

"Sorry," she said meekly while holding her throbbing head. "I had a bad dream."

The driver retrieved his worn handkerchief from his pocket and wiped the stress off his face. "I need a break! Everybody off'a this bus so I can gather my damn nerves and get us to where we goin' safely." He then walked down the aisle toward Harlem with narrowed eyes. "And if *you* feel the need to sleep again, don't!"

"She'll be fine from here on out, sir," Jonas replied for her. He then looked softly over to her. "Won't you?"

"I imagine so," Harlem winced.

As the passengers, including the sisters, gladly exited the bus, Jonas offered gently, "We probably ought to get you walkin' about to make sure you don't have no concussion."

There was open land as far as the eye could see. The sky had begun its colorful transformation as blues twirled with oranges, yellows danced with purples, greens jumped over reds and became every color in between in the process. They were near Richmond, Virginia. Dogwood trees with their white flowers saluted far off in the distance, but in their immediate vicinity acres of grass spotted with yellow daffodils, honeysuckle, and dandelions matched the colors in the sky.

"Sure is pretty, isn't it?" Harlem admired.

Makes me happy to be a free man and alive at that."

Harlem stared out at the crop of bodies milling about in the field as she stepped off the last stair. She was reminded of who she was thanks to a few stares which were rooted in the fame she was trying to escape. Not everyone on the bus knew, but the few from Greensboro who did and hadn't seen her board, caught full sight of her now. She instinctively covered her face.

"You alright, Miss Smith?" Jonas asked.

"Just a horrible headache, is all," she said. "Can we walk over there, away from all these folks?"

Jonas led her to the right where there were a few less people. As they passed alongside the bus, they overheard an overweight man speaking to the driver, "So, we didn't blow no tire?"

The driver pulled up his pants with pride. "No, no we did not. Luckily, my expert driving skills kept us safe, thank you very much. Been driving this bus for years now, through snow, sleet, hail, you name it. I done learned a thing or two 'bout safety."

The overweight man stuffed some chew in his lip and scoffed at Harlem. "Good thang, too, 'cause we'd 'a been a bunch 'a sittin' ducks in a pond out here in this field waitin' for help. Folks 'round here don't take kindly to our kind and woulda swooped down on us like we're nothin' more than road kill."

"You mean, less than road kill," the driver added.

Jonas and Harlem smiled weakly at the men who quieted for a brief moment then huddled and whispered about them as they both strolled by.

"They're right you, know," Jonas added. "I was on a bus going through Mississippi once, and this car full of men passed us and then got the notion to stop the bus by pullin' their shiny new Plymouth in front of the bus. Driver had no choice but t' stop or nearly kill us all. Those men jumped on our bus so fast. I thought for sure I was meetin' my maker that night. Four of 'em. Young, too. Barely in college, I imagined. They walked up an' down the aisle, not one of 'em said a thing. And neither did we. They just glared into each an' every person's colored face makin' sure we knew what they were thinking an' had the power t' do. I tried to look away, myself, but one wasn't havin' that. That man leaned his face into mine so close I could smell the soured milk he had for breakfast on his breath. He pinned my soul down so hard just by lookin' at me. May as well have been outside on the road rasslin.' He had the bluest eyes that I will never forget. And the meanest."

"You must have been terrified," Harlem said.

"Terrified ain't even the beginning, Miss Smith." Jonas looked at her with hurt and anger. Their feet rustled through the dry grass as they walked.

"What happened after that?"

"They simply left the bus an' drove off. Our driver couldn't move at first. Nobody could. Then, like you have to do in times like that, we reminded ourselves to start breathing again!" Jonas chuckled softly as he bent down and pulled a long strand of grass from the earth. He chewed on it as he reminisced. "I think we all scooped our spirits up off the floor, hung 'em back up on the hanger where they belonged and got 'em back in order in the closets of our minds. And we got back to our journey."

Jonas and Harlem circled around the outskirts of the twenty or so passengers who had huddled and formed instant communities with one another as they stretched and yawned and filled their lungs with a borrowed ration of fresh air. The few children skipped and tumbled with each other as their mothers looked on with thankfulness.

"Can we rest here a while?" Harlem asked. "My head feels like a fire alarm is ringin' inside."

Jonas laid down his jacket for her to sit. "Relax and close your eyes a moment."

She complied thankfully then moaned, "Oh, I want to go home."

"Is that Greensboro or New York?" Jonas asked as he glanced at her politely.

"Right now, neither I s'pose. I hope to make New York my new home."

"Starting over?"

"Maybe just gettin' started," Harlem relented as she rubbed her temples, eyes closed.

"I've imagined New York is the place to do that. I had a daughter, *have* a daughter that left for New York..." Jonas trailed off.

Harlem opened her eyes. "And, what did she think of it?"

"Wouldn't know. We had a bit of an argument. She left for New York and I never heard from her again as to whether she made it or not."

"Oh. Well. I'm sure she's fine," Harlem could see he wasn't so sure. "Is that why you're going to New York? To find her?"

"That's what I'm aimin' to do."

"Isn't New York a very large place with so, so many people?"

"That it is. I been lookin' for her for a long time and have done just about everything I've needed to do and could do in order to narrow my search."

"What's her name?" she asked.

"Netta."

"Netta?"

Jonas took out a worn photo of her from his suit pocket and shared it with Harlem. Its fraying edges had been taped together.

Harlem handled the photo delicately. "She's very pretty," Harlem said as she reviewed the young girl staring back at her. The face was round with curious eyes, a stubborn nose, and cheekbones that landed in pleasing symmetry.

"How old is she?" Harlem asked.

"Fourteen in that photo. She's seventeen now. 'Bout to turn eighteen next month."

"Same as me," Harlem said. As she returned the photo to him, he looked away from her. "You've shown this photo to a good amount of folks, haven't you?

He hardly had the strength to nod 'yes'. Instead, he carefully replaced Netta's photo. "Promise me something?"

"I barely know you, Mr. Stewart," Harlem answered.

"Let me know when you get settled in New York," Jonas said as he handed her his calling card.

"I appreciate your concern, but… "

"I've learned that certain people like to prey on a person's vulnerabilities. You're an attractive young woman travellin' alone. I wouldn't want anyone to take advantage of…"

Harlem reviewed his parchment-colored card which was engraved smartly with "Jonas Stewart. Accountant." and placed it in her pocket. She rose, wincing at the throb piercing her temple. "I've learned to take care of myself," she said as she handed him his jacket. "Thank you."

"I didn't mean to offend you, Miss Smith, or suggest in any kind a' way that you were incapable of takin' care of yourself. I was simply offerin', I don't know, some guidance." He drifted off. "I haven't seen my daughter for three years, and I can only hope that someone was good enough to offer her the same advice. Wherever she is."

Harlem softened. She figured maybe she could try to trust this man for however many hours were left in their trip 'til they got to New York. If not for the next three minutes. She reached for his shoulder. "I'm sure someone has been as kind to her as you have been to me."

"Thank you for that," Jonas replied. "Would you like to walk a bit more? Probably better for you. Maybe circle once around these folks and then head back to the bus?"

They walked in silence for a while, both lost in their own thoughts. Harlem watched a crow soar high into the sky and wished she'd had the same freedom. They neared Ruth and Mary. Mary slumped on the grass while Ruth paced with her arms crossed.

"I thought I was goin' to die!" Mary muttered.

"Might have served you right, Mary!" Ruth stopped when she saw Jonas. "Do you see what you've done, Mr. Stewart? My sister cannot hold her liquor. I don't know what sort of sailor you took her for, but she is certainly not that!"

"I meant no harm," Jonas smiled as he jaunted toward Mary and knelt before her. He needed her on his side, after all. "Now did, I? I do believe I said that as we shared our good time together, didn't I, Mary?"

"You did, you did. *I* don't blame you, but she does!" Mary pointed her finger at Ruth sharply. "You know what, sister? This is my last trip."

Jonas felt the tiny hairs on his ears prick up. "Your last trip?"

Ruth advanced quickly to her sister and roughly palmed the top of Mary's head. "Mary."

Mary slapped her hand away, "Ow!"

"Sister Mary, you cannot let this one little scare hinder you from riding on the bus ever again. Right, Mr. Stewart?" Harlem offered with a hesitant smile.

"Right," Jonas agreed as he straightened his vest. "Got to keep on with your journey, especially when y' hit a rough patch."

Harlem looked ahead toward the bus. "Looks like it's our time to get back on." The passengers were forming a loose line to re-board. Harlem rubbed the back of her neck, worried. "I should really get back to my things," she said.

"We all should. Sisters, are you ready?" Jonas asked.

Ruth waved them away angrily. "You two go on ahead. My sister needs a little bit more air."

Jonas guided Harlem on ahead, wishing now that he was a fly so he could catch what was going on behind him.

"Have you lost your god-forsaken mind?!" yelled Ruth.

Jonas looked back quickly. Ruth caught his eye and pulled up on her sister so that Mary righted herself to all fours. She jerked Mary away to a farther distance. Mary stumbled as she tried to catch her balance. "I have not lost my mind, and I was one-hundred and ten percent serious when I said this is my last trip!"

"You need to watch your mouth around strangers. And watch it good," Ruth snapped. "Plus, *sister,* you said that last year!"

"Last year wasn't the twelfth year leading up to the thirteenth year," Mary replied groggily.

"Thirteen has nothing to do with anything!"

"It has everything to do with everything. And this little accident here ain't no *coincidence.*"

"You're just scared."

"Scared? Sure I'm scared." Mary pointed dead at Ruth's nose. "You should be, too."

"Of what?" Ruth swatted Mary's finger away and pushed her aside.

"Transporting fine goods is wrong," Mary taunted as she smoothed her faded cotton dress that had made five of the last twelve trips.

"Well then, that makes you wrong, too."

Mary turned on her heel and walked ahead briskly; her arms punctuating the sky as she spoke. "I will lie up and down the streets a' hell if anyone asks me if I have anything to do with you and your job of bringing girls from ev'ry stretch of these United States to Magdalena. As far as anyone else is concerned, I am your faithful companion and that's it!"

Ruth caught up to her sister and shook her real good. "Faithful companion? I think not. Companions aren't paid. Companions don't lie and steal. You, my dear, are an accomplice. Accept it!"

Ruth had every reason to shake her sister. She'd just about had enough. They were sisters by blood, not Sisters of the Cloth. They were also sisters in crime. It was their business to find unaccompanied girls, no younger than fifteen, and women no older than 30 who had no anchors in life, were of good breed, and who could be taught manners, grace, and style—if they didn't already possess such traits. Ruth didn't always judge a girl by her cover. Just like any good book, the binding might be frayed or the leather on the book may be worn, but that didn't mean the book was bad or couldn't be read. Some girls would have their hair poking about their heads like an old broom. Or they'd be so thin, looked like they could float away in the sky with even the lightest of breeze. Ruth knew these things. They fancied women and girls who looked like they could learn how to dance as Josephine Baker did and could consequently perform nightly for the uptown and downtown elite. They also desired women who were of the malleable ilk who could be forced into having relations with these elite clients in an arrangement that some would call prostitution at Lady Magdalena's Manor in Harlem.

Once Ruth had laid eyes upon Harlem, she knew she'd found their next paycheck. Being a resident of Greensboro, it was hard to not know about the Markeson girl. Ruth figured a girl like her, with a past like hers, was sure to get an itch to leave Greensboro at one point or another. Most folks can't take living day-to-day on the wagging tongues of mouths more twisted than a sidewinder. Bad enough when the wag is coming from a parlor of bored women tucked away on a sunny afternoon. Worse when it's the entire town wagging just as breezy as cotton sheets drying on the line. Ruth knew, whether for a short trip or a very long one, there would be a departure. She was willing to be as patient as necessary, 'cause this girl had some zero's behind her name that made her even more attractive than she already was physically. Never in a million years could she save, win, steal, or even earn the kinda money that Harlem had. Ruth felt it was high time she got a taste of the good life.

"I ain't no accomplice," Mary yelled.

"You might want to recall Arnetta Plummer from Kentucky," she said still shaking Mary.

"Arnetta Plummer?!" Mary, incensed, yelled loudly.

Jonas, who had just helped Harlem onto the bus, heard Mary and stopped cold.

"Somethin' wrong?" Harlem asked.

"No. You go on ahead and make sure your things are safe."

"Do you need some water or something?" She stepped down toward him.

"I'm going to rest out here just a few minutes longer," he smiled faintly. "Go on. I'll be right there."

Ruth covered Mary's mouth with her rough hand and leaned into her sister's tired, freckled face. "Yes. Arnetta Plummer," she hissed.

Jonas watched them from afar. His daughter's name slapped him awake. He lovingly called her 'Netta, but everyone else called her by her full name, which was Arnetta. Their family name was Plummer. For the purposes of finding his daughter, he'd taken on the last name "Stewart" as a protective alias. He knew the sisters were responsible for his daughter's disappearance, he just didn't know to what extent, and he still didn't know where Arnetta was. It took everything in his being to not run and strangle both of the sisters with their tongues as ropes.

Mary yanked Ruth's hand from her mouth. "Arnetta Plummer was a mistake."

"Mistake or not, you were involved."

Mary tried to regain her composure. "I don't care for you much right now."

"I bet you care for that big check that girl has," Ruth baited. For the first time, she'd wished to heaven that she was an only child, 'cause she wasn't feelin' like splittin' nothin' with her baby sister. It had been twelve long years, the two of them doing business, and Ruth wanted this big bonus for herself. She kept thinkin' clear and loud how she could keep the zeros from Mary and the answers that kept comin' up were not Christian-like, and she considered herself a good Christian woman.

"Why didn't you just steal it when you had the chance, Ruth?"

"After everything that girl's been through?"

"Don't pretend like you have that girl's well-being in mind. You want our pay from Magdalena, too," she needled.

"Damn right I want my pay! We put our lives on the line each year to bring her girls that keep her business running." Ruth turned into a bulldog as she barked. "Magdalena makes a profit ten-fold, and we get paid a measly dime in comparison. And we get paid even less respect!"

"Who gives a hoot about respect, Ruth? What about these girls? I've known for a while now that what we're – you're – doin' is wrong. Along the way, I felt like by us taking girls that were orphans or had no more family to speak of, that we were helpin' them out in some kinda way. That has just not been the case lately. And ain't none of it worth it. I'm retiring!"

"Have you ever used your little brain to think of the big picture, Mary?"

Mary crossed her arms, offended. "You should be nicer to me, sister. If it wasn't for my little brain realizing I could get to Harlem Winnepega Markeson's lawyer, who then revealed to me when she was receiving all that money, you would not have had such an easy prospect this year."

"If it wasn't for me finding out Harlem Winnepega Markeson was leaving when she was leaving, we would have lost out on this prospect!"

"Fine, Ruth. Fine!"

Jonas approached the women casually as he and Netta used to do when hunting a rabbit for stew. They were oblivious to him.

"All I know is," Mary continued. "No matter how big that check is, I'm getting half of it and this is my last job with you."

Ruth had no intention of splitting the damn check. But she did still need her sister's help. "We can do what Magdalena does, if not better. She owes us. Hell, the way I figure it, that Manor should be ours! Did you ever think of that?"

Mary was no longer listening. "I'm retiring and my behind is gonna be sittin' on my porch in a rocking chair in year thirteen." Mary was starting to twirl about as she had when she was a child in corn rows.

Ruth followed after her. "Mary."

"And I will be drinkin' fine whiskey..."

Ruth stomped her foot as *she* had done when she was a child in corn rows. "Mary!"

Mary ran backwards, away from the bus. "On ev'ry day that I please!"

Ruth ran through the field to her and started shaking her again, "Mary! Shut up!"

Jonas was upon them, undetected. He cleared his throat. Ruth, quite unaware, released her grip and faced Jonas. Her face looked meaner than if he'd just pushed her into an icy creek on Christmas day.

"Thought I'd let you know it's plumb near time t' go, Sisters"

Ruth kept her grimace as she and Mary slowly looked around and caught on that they were the only ones left in the field. They looked further on at the bus and noticed that just about every window was filled with a brown face staring back at them. The bus driver honked his horn long and hard.

"If'n you need more time," Jonas offered.

He'd been trailing them in Greensboro for this past month once he'd learned of their whereabouts from a private detective he'd hired back home in Kentucky. He'd set himself up in the town as an accountant and from the grocer to the cobbler to the little old ladies having tea, he learned everything he could about Ruth and Mary. The answers were all the same: didn't have much, they kept to themselves, and they left town on vacation once each year to see family in New York for a month. He got incredibly lucky when it turned out that their next prospect was so close to home. He only had to watch and wait. He felt Harlem got lucky too, because he was there to protect her. He knew he could have gone to the police, but he couldn't risk the sisters not telling him where his daughter was. Or the police not believing him. Harlem was bait for all of them, including Arnetta. He prayed that the Lord would forgive him and bless him with the mechanics to keep her safe.

"I don't know what you're up to," Ruth stormed to Jonas. "But you better leave us alone or you will be very, very sorry."

She pushed him out of her way. "C'mon, Mary!"

CHAPTER 6

Harlem removed Jonas's card from her skirt pocket and placed it safely in her pocket book. She clamped the silver ball clasp closed, bought especially for this trip. The white piping along its edges matched her shoes. Harlem then checked her Samsonite to make sure everything was secure, which it was. As she stood to replace her valise in the overhead compartment, she caught the eye of the young boy who'd been so excited to sit next to Jonas. Harlem smiled softly as she spoke to both him and his mother in the seat behind hers. "You two okay?"

The mother rubbed her son's shoulders. "We're fine, thank you."

"I bumped my head," said the little boy. His eyes were large and round as marbles.

Harlem rested her elbows on the back of her seat as she leaned over it to talk to him. "Well now, so did I."

"I cried," he admitted as he nestled his head into his mother's side.

"I did too, a little," Harlem said. "Are we done cryin' now?"

"Yes."

Harlem pinched his cheek, "That's a good boy. I'm done, too."

Ruth, Mary, and Jonas filed down the aisle with Ruth leading the way. The driver started the engine with a scoff as they passed.

Ruth leaned into Jonas' window seat, found his leather attaché, and flung it toward the open seat next to Harlem.

"Mr. Stewart, my sister needs me for this last part of our trip," she said. "I'd kindly like you to sit next to Miss Smith so that I may sit over here."

She policed Mary into the window seat and positioned her own bottom squarely into the aisle seat, staring straight ahead indignantly.

Jonas was about to bring up "The Gout" but knew he simply did not have a choice in the matter. He recovered his attaché and settled in his new seat.

"Have you ever seen a more peculiar pair of sisters?" Jonas whispered jokingly to Harlem.

"No. No I have not," Harlem chuckled.

Several hours later as midnight drew near, the passengers finished up their last game of bid whist, tucked their guitars back in their cases, and allowed themselves to be lulled asleep by the soothing drone of the bus's engine and its subtle rocking from the rotating tires. Soon, most were asleep or near it. Ruth watched Harlem trying her best not to fall into a deep sleep, which had her nodding violently from side to side as she fought years of fatigue.

As soon as Jonas moved deep into his own dreams, Ruth made her move.

She rose quietly and squeezed herself down the aisle to the driver. Ruth whispered urgently in his ear. His close-set eyes looked up in alarm then narrowed in anger as he peered through his rearview mirror back at the sleeping Jonas.

The driver reached behind his chair with one hand while keeping the other on the huge steering wheel and nudged the man behind him. He whispered angrily to him. Ruth added hushed yet vehement commentary where needed. Soon a fire was lit. That man torched another man and he another with the embers sparked by Ruth's calculating tongue. As Ruth made her way back to Mary in the twelfth row of the bus, a blaze burned in her wake.

She sat patiently and basked in the crackling glow of her work like a perfectly toasted marshmallow.

HARLEM'S AWAKENING

CHAPTER 7

"Folks, we'll be arriving into New York City very shortly. Y'all make sure you pick up all your things and leave my bus tidy," the driver instructed, looking back shrewdly to the passengers through his overhead rearview mirror.

The passengers did as they were told as they hopped up to get their suitcases. Their jumpy eagerness to arrive crackled like an egg frying on a skillet. Harlem felt the same.

"I think I'm nervous now. Yes. I am nervous now," she said to Jonas, her voice higher than normal as she fiddled with the pearl-button closure on her gloves.

Jonas gently patted her hands, and smiled. "You'll be just fine, Miss Ann. Just fine."

He stood to get his weathered, rust-colored suitcase from the overhead above Ruth. Jonas peered down at her, hoping to make contact, get more information from her, but her eyes were closed. By the way her short, pressed curls barely rested upon her head rest, he knew she was neither resting nor asleep. As though reading a warning message in Braille, he rubbed his chin and looked about at the passengers. The farmer turned his head quickly when he caught his eye. As soon as Jonas turned away to look at another, he could feel the farmer and those around him returning stares to his direction.

"I'm a touch nervous myself," he said.

Jonas sat and pulled his suitcase forward over his knees to rest solidly on his lap. He double checked that the brass flip hooks were firmly connected. Two years ago, in Memphis, he'd had to run for a connecting bus and the hooks had come a-loose. That day, everyone at the depot had known that his undershorts were embroidered on the seat with a large red heart which lassoed a flowery "J+J." He had more things to worry about right now than his undershorts. He placed his hand over his heart; his flask, albeit light in weight was secure against the silk of his inside suit pocket. He pulled his Fedora securely onto his head. The bumpy worry wrinkles in his forehead made the cotton fibers in the band stretch loudly in response.

"Do you still have my card?" Jonas asked Harlem without looking at her.

"Yes, right here in my pocketbook," she said brightly.

Jonas watched the overweight man lean across the aisle to the farmer.

"Where are you staying, Miss Smith?" he asked Harlem gravely.

"I'm goin' to Harlem," she said to his profile.

When he turned to face her, she saw something in his dark brown eyes that hadn't been there before.

"We're all goin' to Harlem," Jonas said as he stood. Something wasn't right and he knew Ruth was the cause of it.

"Well. At first, until I get settled properly, I'll be at a boarding house on one hundred and twenty fifth street and, and Lenox Avenue," Harlem stammered.

"That sounds fine," Jonas replied as he touched Ruth lightly on her shoulder. She opened her eyes like a cat interrupted while eating a bird. Ruth looked at his hand on her shoulder. He removed it slowly.

"Sister Ruth, I'm pleased I was able t' be in the comp'ny of you an' Sister Mary. Would be my honor t' take you both t' dinner at my favorite restaurant in Harlem. Where'll you be stayin'?"

Mary began to speak but Ruth held her back forcibly. Ruth stared straight ahead and said, "That is a generous offer, Mr. Stewart. But, no thank you."

"Alrighty." He reached into his wallet for his card. "Sister Mary, thank you for sharin' your story with me 'bout lookin' for fine goods. Sure would be somethin' to hear more 'bout that!" He politely reached across Ruth to hand her his card and Ruth smacked it out of Jonas' fingers as she shot daggers at Mary with her eyes.

"Ruth!" Harlem exclaimed.

"That's alright now, Miss Smith." Jonas said. "Ruth is just tryin' to protect her sister is all."

Jonas bent to pick up his card up from the floor which had torpedoed into the aisle. Jonas heard somebody shout, "NOW!" He looked up just in time to see a fist coming square at his jaw, but not enough time to duck it. He reeled backwards, bounced off a seat, and landed flat on his face.

Jonas scrambled to push himself back up. An excruciating blow to his shoulder made him wish he hadn't. He howled at the shock of it, collapsing clumsily onto his chest. Weight dropped violently on his back. His head shot up and he choked for air, his hand slapping for help against the metal leg of a seat like a fish dying on the dirt.

Harlem pushed away from the window she was pinned against but the young army man who had her pinned there pushed back even harder. The roughness of his uniform slid against her chest as his back pressed into her collar bone. She could smell the conch in his straightened hair. She was trapped by it and him.

"Stay back, ma'am!" he ordered.

"Wait! Stop!" Harlem yelled as she tried to lean forward past the man to see Jonas. They had him pinned to the ground like a lassoed calf, and she could only see his feet which were kicking frantically. One of his shoes flew off, and his foot writhed like an eel under the weight of the men.

"Somebody help him!" Harlem yelled. "What's he done?!"

The man holding her turned to her, his panicked dark brown eyes sparked with adrenaline and authority. "He's a fugitive! Wanted back in Greensboro for murder."

Harlem paled. "Murder?!"

"Help! Help me!" Jonas struggled.

From his rearview mirror, the driver watched the melee unfold as he carefully maneuvered the bus into the terminal. He'd had people faint on his bus and once a backwoods dame pulled a quick knife on her own brother, but he'd never had something as sensational as this happen under his watch. He quickly faced his charges.

"Folks, you can see we have here what you call a 'situation,'" he said. "I need y'all to calmly exit the bus so that the men can take care of business."

The men pulled Jonas up to his feet and dragged him the few rows to the back of the bus faster than anything. Then the gossipy buzzing began:

"Murder? We all coulda been killed in our sleep!"

"Fella looked as normal as peach cobbler. Can't trust nobody these days!"

Harlem grabbed her things and jumped into the stream of passengers trying to flee the bus. She didn't dare look back at Jonas. She didn't want to see him, to look into the eyes of a man she started to trust. Harlem felt an urgent hand pushing firmly on the small of her back. Harlem shot her head back, "Hey! I'm just as frightened as you are!" But she soon relaxed, recognizing her pusher.

"Don't worry," Ruth said quickly. "You're safe with us."

HARLEM'S AWAKENING

CHAPTER 8

"I just don't understand!" Harlem said as she, Ruth, and Mary scuttled through the colored waiting room of the bus station. Harlem was thankful to follow Ruth through the horde of tense brown faces pushing past them to the waiting busses at the terminals from which they'd just escaped. A monotone voice echoed over a loud speaker, announcing arrivals and departures, which made it that much harder to hear Ruth.

"You can never be too sure of folks, now can you?" Ruth tossed over her shoulder.

"I'm very surprised myself!" Mary added.

"But, his daughter. He has a daughter," Harlem jumped out of the way of a tall man carrying a large suitcase above his head.

"Hurry, Ann," Ruth said, not exactly hearing her. "You'll be swallowed up and we'll never find you!"

Ruth continued to plow confidently toward the door with Mary in tow. Harlem shut her mouth and did as she was told. She could see light ahead, spilling through a door above a throng of hats and feathers on hats. She swallowed to keep her heart from jumping through her throat.

Harlem was actually pushed through the doors to the outside more than she felt she walked through them. As she landed on two feet, her mouth dropped wide open.

Harlem gasped as she slowly leaned her head back, holding her hat in place. The gray concrete building in front of her seemed to grow taller and taller, almost as if its pointy tip was just about to puncture the sky. And it wasn't the only one to do so.

As Harlem walked backwards to see more, she bumped into a woman in a smart gray tweed suit who was having a lively conversation with another woman in a darker suit with a long, fitted skirt.

"Hey, watch it, Sister," the cosmopolitan woman shouted.

"Pardon me!" Harlem exclaimed as she watched the woman fold her arms, her thin pocket book dangling from its delicate strap laced on her arm. She spun around and was met with a wall of strangers. Harlem spun away from them and fled into the chest of a young man with light gray eyes, a thin mustache and a square jaw. She could smell his woodsy after shave. He nodded slightly at her and seemed to forget he'd done so just as quickly, as he kept walking. Harlem had never been that close to a white man before. Cabs and cars honked like sirens, adding to her cocoon of confusion. "Mary? Mary!" she cried out with her hands cupped at her mouth.

"Yoo-hoooo! Yooo-hooo!" She turned to see Mary waving a white handkerchief at her. Harlem exhaled. Some of the bats in her stomach fluttered back into butterflies. She waved back. Mary stood at the curb with Ruth in line with the rest of the colored folks waiting for a taxi. Harlem attempted to make her way toward them through the swift current of worker ants scurrying from one point to another. She was very much in the way, with both suitcases in hand and her handbag wedged under her arm.

A passerby hurriedly bumped into her shoulder with such force she stepped out of her T-strap. She quickly tried to catch her balance while using her suitcases like the weights of a scale and touched her toes on the sidewalk to field for her shoe. Her toes, protected only by a silk stocking, were left defenseless amongst the hard soles of Oxfords and peep-toe pumps pounding the pavement. Her big toe got in the way of someone's purpose and she roared, "OWWW!" A young brown-skinned woman with the brightest hazel eyes and dragging a small girl by the hand paused to make sure Harlem wasn't being assaulted. She huffed about being inconvenienced and then continued on her way.

Harlem was a ping-pong ball while hopping back and forth to get her shoe back on. As she hopped, her handbag fell from beneath the crook of her arm. The Hatch & Hatch envelope fell from the purse and was swept into the mini tornado of folks sidestepping and doe-si-doe-ing one another. Ruth darted after it. She rescued it easily, surprising herself. With it in hand, she looked at Mary, who was talking to a handsome gentleman in the taxi line. She hadn't seen a thing. Ruth looked toward Harlem, who hadn't yet seemed to notice she'd even lost the envelope.

Harlem followed her lipstick as it rolled under the black pump of a woman walking so fast that Harlem thought there was a fire somewhere. The woman's full yellow skirt of small, black polka dots twirled as she spun about, looking down to see on what she'd nearly broken her neck. She scooped to pick it up, handed it to Harlem, tossed, "Here ya go, honey," and twirled back on her way. Harlem caught it happily and gathered her suitcases once more.

Ruth held the envelope. "Oh my God," she thought fast. She was near a mailbox and used it to hide. She opened the envelope. "Oh my GOD!" she bellowed. A man turned and looked at her. Ruth smiled and walked away from him, stuffing the check back in its envelope. She kept walking past Harlem. Away from Mary. Away from everything that made her hate how she lived and breathed.

"Ruth!" she heard. She didn't care. She kept walking.

"Ruth! Where are you going?" It was Mary. "Ruth!"

Ruth stopped.

Mary spun her around. "What are you doing? Where're you going so fast?"

For once, Ruth was speechless. She stared at everything and saw nothing. She heard nothing. She felt free. She felt—

Mary grabbed the envelope from her. "Ruth?"

Honking, a siren, people talking—each filled Ruth's head like helium. She never remembered the city being so loud. "I found it. I was…" Ruth trailed off.

Harlem arrived breathless. "You all can't leave me like that!" She hissed. "What were you thinking?" Harlem reprimanded both women as though she were the one in charge. She looked at Mary. "Mary?"

"Here. You dropped this."

Harlem paled. She looked in her purse to confirm the check wasn't there. "My good God. Thank you, Mary." Harlem hugged Mary with all her might. "Thank you. You saved my life. You absolutely saved my life."

"Don't mention it," Mary said as she stared at Ruth.

Harlem firmly placed the check in her purse. She jammed the clutch back under her arm and scooped her suitcases. "I have got to get a pocket book with a strap!"

Ruth walked away from them. "You're lucky my sister found it, Miss Ann."

Harlem followed Ruth back to the cab line where Ruth jumped into the front of the line and stole the first cab from a small man by pushing him aside.

"I have the gout and I need a cab right this minute!" Ruth shouted in the face of the frightened man.

"Well, if you need to have it that bad," he said.

"C'mon Mary!" Ruth yelled over his head.

Harlem ran for the cab. "Mary, we have t' go! C'mon."

Ruth jostled Harlem into the cab while Mary ran around and entered through the other door, slamming it. "Sister Ruth. Really! I'm not a sack of potatoes," Harlem exclaimed, flanked between the two.

"Forgive me, your highness. I just wanted to get us into this cab quickly before someone else got it," Ruth replied.

"Your highness?"

Mary leaned in. "My sister thinks she's a lamb when she's really an ox."

Ruth snorted. "Really, Mary."

"And she thinks I'm as stupid as one," Mary scoffed to herself as she looked out the window.

"'Your highness,' I simply asked to not be rough housed."

"I'd hoped you could take a joke," Ruth said as she reviewed Harlem's clothes, trying hard not to compare them to the worn threads she wore.

"We all come from the same place, Ruth," Harlem said as she rubbed her toe.

"No, we don't," Ruth sniffed as she looked out her window.

Harlem chose to ignore her because she wasn't quite sure why Ruth would say something so mean. She looked ahead and allowed herself to be mesmerized by the offerings of the city's landscape, its people, and how its concrete edges seemed to hedge them all inside like a box. Having been used to fields and acres of land that extended as far as the eye could see, there were so many things to look at here that Harlem didn't know what to look at first. She forgot about the sisters and wished her mother were with her in the cab instead; wished she could squeeze her mother's thin hand to share and release some of the excitement that was exploding within. Harlem wished she could look into her mother's gentle eyes for comfort and safety and ask as many questions as her mind could conjure. She wished so many things.

George had said New York was some kind of wonderful and how he'd hoped she'd find the happiness she'd been missing. Right about now, Harlem didn't even know what happiness actually looked like. She knew she wanted new thoughts to grow: bright pink, gold, peach, teal, and copper ones that hadn't been slithered on by any dirty, slimy snake.

"Oh, my!" Harlem shot up. "In the rush I hadn't stopped to think of where I'm even going!"

Harlem pulled her new leather address book from her valise, and flipped through its alphabetically marked pages to the letter "S." She looked at the only entry on the stark white page. She'd neatly written it there herself just three weeks ago during a meeting with Mr. Hatch. He'd made the recommendation based on a written response he'd received from a second cousin who'd visited New York.

"Driver, could you stop at Stonewall Room and Board at four-twenty," she said.

Ruth interrupted Harlem with a tap on the thigh. "Where are our manners? Now Miss Ann, we just so very much assumed that you would absolutely love to stay with us at Lady Magdalena's Manor."

The cab swerved unexpectedly to avoid a pedestrian. "Sorry there, ladies." The driver called back to them. Harlem lifted herself from Mary's shoulder and steadied her hat as it had fallen over her eyes on the swerve.

"Thank you, but I've mine own arrangements."

Ruth placed her hand on Harlem's arm. "Stonewall Room and Board? But I'm certain Lady Magdalena's Manor is much nicer than your boarding house."

The cab driver smirked and pulled his cap low. Ruth told him to be quiet with her eyes as they connected in the rearview mirror.

"You will love Lady Magdalena's. She treats you like family," Mary said, still scowling.

Ruth crossed her arms over her black rectangular pocketbook. "I suggest we concentrate on getting Miss Smith to suitable accommodations. We had a small hiccup with getting this far. I apologize for that. Let's move on."

"Move on? Yes, let's," Mary said.

"Now, Miss Smith, Lady Magdalena's has the best biscuits in town. But, I imagine, tea would be more to your liking?"

"Tea?" Harlem looked between the two women.

"I should add Lady Magdalena has plenty of rooms and would find it a pleasure to board someone as lovely as you," Ruth campaigned.

"Yep," Mary said.

Harlem put her gloved hand on the seat and leaned forward to speak with the driver. "I appreciate the invitation, but it's all been arranged for me."

Ruth gently pulled Harlem back. "You'll have a choice, then. Come see the Manor. If you like it, you can keep your arrangement for this evening and transfer to the Manor tomorrow. Agreed?"

"Listen, I've said, 'No.' I can't be any more polite than that." She forcibly leaned forward again. "Driver. Driver! Let me out, please."

The driver, with graying hair at his temples and seemingly in his early sixties, with skin the color of candied pecans, looked back at her through his rearview mirror.

"I can't much stop right here for you, Miss," he said. "You won't be able to get another cab straight away in this neighborhood."

"Well, that just doesn't make any sense in a city this big!" Harlem pounded both palms on the partition.

"Shhh. Shhh. Dear. Relax. I'm sorry. We were only trying to help your transition to New York to be that much better. You can't fault us for wanting to help one of our own, now can you?" Ruth said.

Mary laughed aloud.

"We just got a little too excited, that's all. Please forgive us. Now, we're already in this cab and getting another can be a time, as the driver just said. Let's share it and all will be fine. We'll drop you at your location and continue on to ours. Agreed?"

"Fine," Harlem sighed.

Ruth slowly smiled at her with a wide toothy grin. Harlem flinched at the oddity of it. Her teeth were unusually small and pointy, something between those of a wolf and an alley cat.

"Driver, please take us on to…"

"Lenox Avenue. 125th street," Harlem answered.

HARLEM'S AWAKENING

CHAPTER 9

They arrived in front of a brick building the color of dirty, wet sand. The building was connected to several others of differing shades of brown, creating one long train of homes that took up the entire block. There wasn't a lick of grass to be seen.

The building had three levels and all nine windows had folks hanging out of them. Some yelling at the people walking down the street or yelling to each other. Some just sitting there alone like they were a frog watching butterflies go by. The porch stairs were flanked by two short walls reminding Harlem of an armchair. A man of about twenty stood on the sidewalk in front of the porch. At least he was trying to. He was using the arm rest to prop himself up.

Harlem couldn't see his eyes because his hat was smashed down low around his face. Maybe he put it there or maybe someone put it there for him. She watched him as his back slid along the wall to his right, bending sideways at his waist, and when his knees buckled to catch him from falling, he jumped up so fast and straight seemed like he was launching himself into outer space. Then he'd lean over to the other side and it would happen all over again.

He wasn't the only one in front of the building. The unfamiliar and peculiar things she watched filled her with excitement and dismay as she leaned over Mary and clutched the metal door handle of the open window. She heard music that jumped from somewhere unknown. The music was wild and energetic; it bounced off the building, the people, and the cab. A woman with skin like a stick of butter rubbed herself on the lap of a fella so slow and low, seemed she was about to melt right there on his lap. He held onto her hips while she dipped and oozed rhythmically. Harlem thought they must not have heard the same music that the dancing folks on the sidewalk heard because those folks were hopping up and down and over each other like cold water on a hot griddle.

Harlem's hand went to her throat. "My," she said. George said Harlem USA was full of people trying to forget stuff and, yes, she wanted to be around them, but she wondered if this was what he meant?

"Don't these people work?" Harlem remarked to herself.

"Some yes, overnight mostly. This is their night time," Ruth answered.

"This brownstone is jumpin,'" Mary remarked with interest as they looked at the spectacle before them. She bent her head as if in prayer, snapped her fingers and wiggled her bottom in her seat to the bouncy rhythm. She stopped and placed her hands in her lap when she saw both Harlem and Ruth staring at her like she was crazy.

"This brownstone is… jumpin'," Harlem repeated in awe. She had never even heard of a brownstone let alone seen it "jump."

"This isn't quite what I expected," Harlem said, trying to hide her disappointment.

Ruth leaned over to her and whispered, "Lady Magdalena's is much, much quieter."

"Nicer," Mary added.

"For someone such as yourself," Ruth finished.

"Ladies. The meter is runnin'..." The cabbie turned around and reminded.

Harlem stared out the window and reviewed the extravaganza before her. She was looking for some place to belong, but certainly *this* wasn't the place. When the young man's knees buckled for the last time and he actually fell into a disoriented heap and the dancers whooped with glee, she acquiesced. "I guess I haven't a choice, do I?" Her hand released the handle of the cab's back door and she settled back between the sisters.

"Magdalena's Manor," Ruth said as she gave the address.

The cab driver turned, put his elbow over the partition, and eyed them suspiciously. "I know where it's at, lady. I wasn't born yesterday."

"Well. Aren't we that much more fortunate," Ruth replied as she glared at him. He turned around and focused on the road.

Shortly, the cab pulled curbside to an unassuming Brownstone. Much nicer. Much quieter. Except for its carved heavy oak door with a wrought-iron door-knocker the shape of a coiled snake, Harlem thought the building looked like any of the other buildings on this nice, quiet block.

HARLEM'S AWAKENING

CHAPTER 10

Honey, a soulful, young woman of twenty-three who looked like her name, knelt down to Tilda, a sixteen-year-old girl with smooth coconut brown skin who was very small for her age.

There wasn't a lot of time for words, so Honey used what time and syllables she had wisely and bravely.

"Haven't I always taken care of you?" she asked with a steady voice.

Tilda trembled. She'd been scared before, but not as scared as she felt right now. She nodded quickly.

Honey's compassionate green eyes soothed Tilda's as she unclasped a delicate gold necklace from her own neck and gently placed it around Tilda's neck. The letter "A" dangled from it. Tilda touched the small charm hesitantly. It was also of gold, although time had tarnished its original grandeur and it was now dull and flat in color. Still, she thought it was beautiful. Honey affectionately positioned the lettered charm in the center of Tilda's petite chest, "This 'A' is for 'Always'."

"I'll still be right here with you, always." Honey hugged Tilda with all her might as if to seal in the promise she'd just made.

In some ways, Tilda could have been her sister, their bond was so tight. Tilda had been left on Honey's family's front porch when she was about five-months old. Honey had been nearly seven then and had been asked to fetch the milk from the porch and there, next to their morning delivery, was Tilda bundled tightly in a man's overcoat and nestled in a packing crate. Her name had been penciled in perfect penmanship on a scrap of newspaper and pinned to the tattered tweed. That was the only information they'd ever had on her. It was all they ever needed. Honey's family had been well-off then, before the market crash, and both her good-hearted parents reasoned that if someone was desperate enough to leave their innocent child with them then it was their duty through God to take care of that child. Based on the care that had been taken to write her name on the note, they assumed Tilda came from good stock and that she truly was a teeny blessing in disguise.

Honey cradled Tilda's head between her light golden-brown hands and smoothed Tilda's two fuzzy cornrows. Honey had not the time to re-do the braids this morning, and now, who knew when or if she'd ever be able to do them again. They looked sadly at one another before Tilda grabbed Honey one more time in a gripping bear's hug as they crouched in the Manor's foyer, just outside the heavy oak pocket doors. Suddenly the doors slid open.

"Honey!" Magdalena yelled as she charged through the doors. In the dim light of the foyer, she nearly tripped over them. "God dammit! Didn't you hear me calling for you?!"

Magdalena grabbed Honey by the shoulder and pulled her into the expansive dining room. Tilda followed behind until Magdalena roughly pushed her back, "You stay."

Magdalena's long black hair was alive with anger as she whipped Honey toward her office. Magdalena favored her father in that her skin was the color of a bar of soap. She had his high cheekbones which were characteristic of his French mother and German father. Her long legs carried her to a height taller than most men and her slim frame moved like the branches of a willow tree. Her pale green eyes were ruthless and matched the quality of her heart. She was very much the opposite of Honey, her baby sister, who was golden yellow-brown with hair the color of raw sugar which hardly ever enjoyed the freedom from the tight bun she kept it in. No one knew they were sisters. There were lots of things people didn't know about them. Magdalena needed it that way. Over the years, she learned to orchestrate a symphony of lies because her life depended on their existence.

"Magdalena, you can't do this," Honey warned. "What would mother say?"

"Mother is dead," Magdalena said. With her hand on the door knob to the office, Magdalena looked Honey over with disgust. "Get yourself together."

Honey tugged at the darted bodice of her pale-blue dress and tried to straighten the narrow belt at her waist. The cotton-covered buckle had become so worn in its casing that the tooth jutted out crookedly and wouldn't let the belt lie properly. She wiped the tears from her eyes and consoled her quivering lips with her fingertips to harbor her sobs. Magdalena stormed in and took her position behind a massive ebony desk that had been their father's when he was still with them and they were a family. They weren't alone.

The man in one of the two brown leather armchairs in front of her desk sat motionless.

Magdalena eagerly picked up her smoldering cigarette from the heavy crystal ashtray deeply etched along its edges with designs that reminded her of a wavy sheet of music. She stood with one arm circling her waist and the other busy propping her hand to hold her cigarette, which she brought to her blood-red lips. She narrowed her almond-shaped eyes at her sister.

Honey's chest heaved rapidly. She lifted her chin bravely.

Magdalena turned her back to Honey and the seated man. Her back was thinner than last year, noticeable by the low dip in her velvet gown. Magdalena ate more last year, made more money last year. This year was different; earnings were less and it was Honey's fault. Magdalena perched her thin bottom on the edge of the desk and focused on her cigarette's burning tip as she drew long and hard from it. Watching the tiny shards of tobacco perish in a crackling blaze summoned by her deep inhale kept her insides at bay.

She quickly blew out a stream of smoke high toward the coffered ceiling. Her parrot, a bartered gift, released a shrill whistle in protest. It was nestled off in a corner, trapped in a cage two sizes too small. She often felt like that bird and had no sympathy for it, just as no one had any for her. Magdalena rubbed out her cigarette in the depths of the crystal ashtray and flicked her butt at it.

"Shut up, bird," she said.

Magdalena sat. Her strong fingers gripped the sturdy wood arms of the chair as she rolled it forward, closer to the desk. As she did so, her hair, darker than midnight, formed a hooded velvet cloak about her oval face and statuesque shoulders. Magdalena slowly shifted her gaze directly in front of her and smiled with cunning charm at Otto, a shifty, greasy man whose face and complexion looked like cold oatmeal.

"Now. Where were we?" she inquired while seductively licking her thumb to count a large stack of bills that had been left interrupted on her desk.

"Dunno. You tell me." Hair oil stained his collar as he twisted his neck to look back at Honey. He rose from his chair and, in false ceremony, he pulled his ratty vest down over his soiled shirt as though he were a respected banker. He shuffled to Honey and reviewed her like the meat he hung downtown at the shipping yards to be stamped and graded before it was sold to the highest bidder. He straightened his worn leather belt and shoved his rough hands into his pockets.

"Dees one better be better dan d' last one, Magdalena," he muttered as he sucked his dingy teeth.

"*Lady* Magdalena," she corrected as she rubber banded the first stack of money.

"You and I both knows you ain't no fuckin' lady."

"As if I, or anyone else, gives a flying fig about your opinion, Otto."

"Fuck you. An', like I said, if dees one ain't better dan d' last one, my bosses are gonna…"

Magdalena surveyed Honey. Their matching green eyes bore holes into the other. "This one is special," Magdalena said.

"Maggie…please," Honey tried once more.

Otto pulled out a pocket knife and began to clean his dirty nails. "Why is she talkin'?" he asked.

Magdalena glared at Honey. "I didn't hear anything." She pulled a rubberband around the second stack of money.

The morbid suggestion of Otto's knife scraping against his jagged nails filled the room. Honey wiped her forehead as she took in her father's office. She used to feel so safe here. *"This will help you concentrate, papa," she'd said braiding his long grey beard while he poured over his work.*

"I can concentrate when I have provided for my family my shayna punim." He would say, patiently allowing her to continue. He worked himself to death providing for them.

Honey gazed at the empty space above the fireplace where his portrait once lived. Now, the portrait was in the office's back closet where Magdalena stowed many reminders of their past. Honey closed her tired eyes and tried to recall his warm hazel eyes one last time.

The doorbell chimed ominously through the Manor, startling all of them. Honey's eyes popped wide open as Magdalena looked at her watch.

"They're early," she said. Magdalena finished with the third stack of bills and quickly shoved it all into a hidden drawer in the desk.

Magdalena walked out.

Otto grabbed Honey's arm. "Maggie!" she cried.

"Shuddup, you," Otto threatened as he dragged Honey through the dining room toward the front door. Honey pulled back, digging her heels into the carpet. She was on the losing end of Otto's tug of war. She grappled at the high-backed dining-room chairs, knocking them to the ground like weary fallen soldiers unable to defend themselves against a sudden ambush. From the shadows, Tilda watched.

"Tilda!" Honey shouted, her eyes as large as the moon. Tilda ran to her and gripped Honey's arm desperately.

"Hey, get outta here," Otto elbowed Tilda aside and pulled Honey to his shoulder like a side of pork. Tilda fell to all fours and reached out for Honey's hand.

"Take care of the others," Honey wept. Tilda scrambled to her feet as she nodded in response.

As they arrived at the foyer, Magdalena looked back at Otto, appalled.

"Put her down!" she said. "They'll see you."

Otto pulled out his pocket knife and pricked it into Honey's side before setting her on her feet. Honey got the message loud and clear. She squealed to let him know.

"Dees little piggy went to market," he grunted.

Magdalena winced ever so slightly; her distaste for the situation was virtually undetectable to others, but her knee-caps, her barometers of conscience, were on fire. Rubbing her knees, she barked, "Watch it!"

"Awww, shuddup," Otto responded.

His cold, greasy hand tightened about her small wrist as they reached the front door. Honey was a sacrificial lamb being led to slaughter. To let him take her from the house would be the end of her; she found the strength to wrench her arm from his. She screamed and she felt her shoulder burn as he whipped her arm behind her back. Terrified, Honey pummeled Otto with her free hand.

"Let me go!"

Suddenly, Honey couldn't feel the ground. She looked down and her feet dangled helplessly. Otto's face came near hers. He had her by the neck. She slapped at his thick arm, unable to breathe.

Magdalena froze.

"You betta behave or yous gonna be sorry," Otto said. Honey was turning blue.

"Put her down," Magdalena whispered. "Or you can't have her."

Otto complied.

Magdalena smoothed her dress. Otto shifted his vest. Honey fell against the wall and gasped grotesquely for air, waiting for it to reach her lungs. When it finally did, and the foyer fell quiet, Magdalena asked, "Everyone ready now?" She turned, not waiting for an answer. Once again, Otto grabbed Honey's hand. This time, she did not resist.

Magdalena opened the majestic door to find Ruth and Mary standing on the doorstep with her new tenant.

CHAPTER 11

Magdalena inspected Harlem with the expertise of a jeweler. She was pleased with the cut of the specimen.

"Sisters! You lovely darlings. You're back." Magdalena hugged Mary briefly and Ruth even more briefly all while staring at Harlem.

Harlem smiled humbly as they gawked at her. She felt as though she was on stage in front of an expectant audience who'd needed immediate reassurance that they'd better not have overpaid their ticket price. The white woman before her with striking black hair, whom she assumed was the 'Magdalena' Ruth and Mary spoke so highly of, may as well have been the beaming stage spotlight, the way she stared. To break her stage fright—instead of breaking into a circle of *pirouettes*—she was about to offer, "How do you do," to the lady, when a white man roughly pushed through the women and rushed passed all of them. He held the hand of a young woman who seemed close to her own age, but lighter in color. The girl looked terrified. Harlem recognized that fear and couldn't take her eyes off her. The girl, her eyes of sea foam green, stared back at her hauntingly.

The man looked like he lived under a rock and consequently ate whatever dank fare he found there. She held her things tightly and moved aside as they passed. He muttered, "Guhd'ay." Harlem stared after them.

"Please, please dears, come in," Magdalena called out. Harlem kept her eyes on them walking down the sidewalk as she herself was coerced inside.

Harlem found herself nestled in an alcove with an umbrella stand and a mirrored armoire which reflected the light from the room just a few feet away. Her family home in Greensboro had one similar. Ruth reached behind Harlem and locked the main front door with a smile while Mary helped her through this area and into the foyer of the Manor.

Harlem hesitated under the high ceilings and dark mahogany molding in this stark entryway. An expansive staircase with a winding oak banister loomed to her right; it matched the two closed sliding pocket doors to her left. In front of her was a white wall which was the backdrop to a round-back armchair. Parallel to the chair was a broom closet door underneath the stairs. The room was fairly large in its own right, but everything felt very square and narrow compared to her expansive home. She wondered what George would think of it. She stepped on a massive oriental rug and noticed in some places the pattern was lost. As she looked up from the deteriorating rug, she was faced with an audience again. She tugged at her gloves nervously and wondered if that cab driver was still outside.

Ruth spoke first.

"Miss Ann, this is Lady Magdalena." Ruth smiled that odd, toothy grin again.

Harlem politely removed her glove, walked forward and offered her hand to Magdalena, who looked liked she'd lived several lives and was maybe thirty-five or forty years old. Their eyes met and her carefully painted, red lips stretched into a smile which revealed very nice, white teeth. Harlem looked closer and collected that Magdalena's face was dusted with light powder; her almond-shaped eyes framed by lids shaded with smoky color that made her look very sophisticated and clever. Her dark eyebrows were shaped and plucked in a stunning arch that Harlem found impressive. Her green eyes, similar to the other girl's green eyes, matched her silk flowing gown. It seemed a bit formal for pre-noon, but Harlem liked such fashionable statements. It reminded her of her mother. Harlem liked the essence of this woman somehow.

"I'm Ann. Ann Smith," Harlem offered.

"Darling, I don't care what your name is! You are simply exquisite," Magdalena said this as she held Harlem's hand and looked to Mary and Ruth with what seemed like intense satisfaction. "You must stay at my Manor."

The closer Harlem looked at this woman's round nose, slightly fuller lips and broad cheek bones, she realized this woman wasn't white at all. She was just very, very light-skinned. Harlem was certain Magdalena was definitely black because she looked just like her Grandma McCormick on her mother's side. Harlem remembered walking into the drug store with Grandma McCormick when she was about six. The store had been in the white part of town. They'd gone there to get some medicine for Grandpa McCormick that wasn't carried in their own part of town. Grandma McCormick had decided to use her "advantage," as she called it, to get what they needed. She walked into that store and immediately started handing things from the shelves to Harlem: soap, face powder, salt... Some of the folks whispered about what this white woman was doing with a negro child, but then figured Harlem was the help. Back on their side of town, everyone knew her grandma was the wife of Shefford McCormick, who was a very prominent banker. Out here, they didn't know her from Mary. Her grandma got the medicine, and they quickly got out of there. Harlem wondered if Magdalena was using her "advantage" or not. And whether Ruth and Mary knew what she knew. Either way, she felt a bit more at ease. She wasn't used to white people and often assumed that white people weren't used to her neither.

"What shall I do with my bags?" Harlem asked.

"Leave them, dear. Tilda will get them," Magdalena said.

Harlem looked around for whomever "Tilda" might be, but no one came.

"Tilda?" Harlem asked.

"She's our help here. She was just here." Magdalena looked around, suddenly the sliding doors opened. "Ah, there, that is Tilda."

Harlem looked to the doors, and standing there at attention was the smallest girl she'd ever seen. She wore a simple, white cotton frock with a light, crisscrossed-patterned apron over it. Her socks were neatly folded at the ankle, but her ankles swam in the stretched out socks. Her brown shoes were scuffed but revealed no holes.

"Are you sure you can manage?" Harlem smiled at her, but the girl looked down and then walked right past her to her suitcases, which were easily half the girl's size. The girl descended upon them and picked them up like they were full of feathers rather than her past. Harlem watched the girl walk up the stairs with the bags and disappear at the top. Harlem figured the girl would return for Ruth and Mary's bags, which she spotted near the foyer door.

"She's awfully strong," Harlem joked.

"Tilda has been taking care of my girls for a long time," Magdalena offered.

"And who was that girl just now? Poor thing looked scared to death," Harlem asked as she turned back to the women.

Ruth and Mary looked to Magdalena, who quickly swept her bejeweled arm into the dining room.

"She rooms here," Magdalena said. "She was terrified, poor thing. She was in horrible pain. Impacted something or other."

"Sounds ghastly," Harlem said. She'd wanted to sound sophisticated, be sophisticated. She'd heard Mrs. Whitscomber use the phrase before and felt this was the perfect time to use it.

"Absolutely ghastly," she repeated.

"Yes, it was." Magdalena sauntered into the dining room. "That man is a troll the dentist sends to strong arm patients who are simply too stubborn to accept what's good for them."

Harlem walked into the room, removed her hat and steadied her curls. "Hopefully she'll be better off soon."

Magdalena stopped. "What'd you say?"

"Just that hopefully she'll be better off soon."

"Yes, I'm sure she will be," Magdalena replied absently. She stopped and leaned forward on one of the dining room chairs Honey had knocked over and Tilda had righted not more than ten minutes ago.

"Lady Magdalena, are you alright?" Harlem asked as Ruth and Mary watched on suspiciously.

"My knees. I do believe it's going to rain."

"Hmmf," Ruth, under her breath, responded. They never knew what Magdalena had up her sleeve. Neither of them trusted her farther than they could throw her. They sat on the far side of the large, gleaming oval maple table. A silver tea-service set for four with fine china graced the center.

Tilda magically appeared with a plate of biscuits.

"Well, where'd you come from?" Harlem exclaimed.

"My Manor is full of twists and turns. You'll see."

Tilda handed Mary the biscuits. "What, am I the biscuit lady now?" Mary clanged down the platter of biscuits and Ruth looked at her disapprovingly. Ruth picked up the tray and walked it closer to Harlem while Magdalena ushered Harlem into a chair.

"Please, sit here, darling."

Harlem sat. Her fingers ran along its dark purple, silk brocade. Harlem reviewed the rest of the room before her with its rich magenta curtains, matching parlour lamps next to cream-linen wing-backed chairs in the four corners of the room, and hanging tapestries.

"You have similar tastes to my mother," she said.

"Oh? Your mother?" Magdalena stopped and looked at Ruth and Mary. "What's she like?"

"Deceased," Harlem said.

"Sorry to hear that. Your father must—"

"Also deceased." Harlem had no intention of talking about or thinking about Roy, so she looked for anything to distract and cut off the thoughts that were starting to snake in her mind. She looked up and noticed an especially spectacular crystal chandelier and quickly blurted, "Oh!" She swore she saw the crystals move. Swore she heard the clink she never wanted to hear again. Swore she felt her body rock from being used. That she was back to counting the clicking sounds of the chandelier, back in her bedroom. Twenty-one, twenty-two, twenty-three. She grabbed the arms of the chair to stop the rocking. Her insides fought to escape up and through her throat.

"Are you alright?" Ruth asked. They didn't get their full pay if a girl had an ailment.

"Yes. Fine." Harlem mustered as she ran her hands along the table, seeking strength from it. "That chandelier...is..."

"It's magnificent! Thank you," Magdalena beamed. "My father had it shipped here from Germany. His grandfather made it."

"I see," Harlem answered. Her chest heaved as she tried to catch her breath. Roy had followed her to Harlem. She had no idea how she was going to shake him, but she knew she couldn't let him get her every time she looked at a piece of glass. Harlem shook her head as she scooched her chair forward.

"Breathe," she said to herself. Methodically, she laid her hat and gloves on the chair next to her and placed her pocketbook in front of her.

"Breathe." She removed a folded linen napkin from her place setting and positioned it on her lap before reaching humbly for a biscuit.

"Breathe!" She exhaled. She was back.

Harlem smiled pleasantly and took a bite and immediately wished she hadn't. Even with the mildly sweet taste and hint of almond, it was the driest piece of sawdust she'd ever had mind to eat, and that was saying a lot. She tried to swallow it, but with the little bit of spit that she'd had left in her mouth, it had turned the biscuit into gunk. It was stuck. Her eyes started to water. She emitted as lady-like a cough as she could, but she knew she sounded like a wounded giraffe. No one seemed to notice, fortunately. Magdalena was coming toward her with the tea pot, but she was taking her sweet time. Harlem buried her face in her napkin to hide the tears springing from her eyes and to suppress the giraffe cackle. Meanwhile, Ruth pushed her teacup and saucer away from her as she placed her elbows on the table and zeroed in on the pocketbook.

"I cannot believe you tried to leave...!" Mary mouthed silently. Her eyes blazing with accusation.

"What?" Ruth looked back at her with raised eyebrows.

Mary curtly nodded her head sideways toward the clutch. *"Don't pretend."*

"Shut up, Mary." Ruth darted back with furrowed brow and pursed lips.

Magdalena watched them from the corner of her eye as she finally poured Harlem some tea.

"Thank you," Harlem gurgled as she sipped the tea.

"You're very welcome," Magdalena said over Harlem's bent head. She glared at the handbag and then at the sisters who caught her drift then quickly looked away.

"Yes," Mary chose to look up to the ceiling and said, "That is a fine chandelier. It's from where, you said?"

Magdalena slowly walked behind Harlem's chair and back toward her seat at the head of the table. Her office door was slightly ajar. She heard the parrot squawk as it worked to interrupt them. With her right hand, she pulled the door closed and turned the knob until she heard it click securely into the latch.

"Germany," she responded while setting the teapot back on the tray.

"How'd you get to Germany?"

She reached for a biscuit from the forlorn tray as she sat demurely. "I didn't. My grandfather shipped it from Germany." She broke the biscuit in two and left the pieces on her plate.

"How'd your people get to Harlem," Mary asked innocently as she fumbled for a cube of sugar from the tea service and popped it in her mouth. "Harlem is full of colored folks, why your people come here?"

"My family has been in Harlem for over thirty years, Mary— "

"Our third cousin came up here in, what was that, 1905 or so, thanks to that negro real estate fella who started buying up everything." Mary quickly chomped the cube into bits so she could finish talking. "From what I remember, all your people left, thought the property up here in Harlem was useless. But then that fellow was quick and ruthless about getting buildings and filled 'em with colored folks. Why'd your people stay?"

Magdalena frowned. "Why wouldn't we stay. My father had every right to be here. Yes, he was a Jew, it that's what you mean by 'my people', Mary. He worked and purchased this home fair and square. And of course now I own it. Of course we got to stay.

Ruth lowered her head into her hands, eyes closed, and shook her head.

Magdalena reached for the tea and began to pour Mary a full cup.

"Hmm. I always wondered that about you Magdalena. So many of you all left or were forced out, but yet, here you are." Mary reached for the cup and brought it to her lips but stopped to say, "Just as content as can be."

Ruth popped her head up upon realizing she'd heard the tea trickle into Mary's cup. Harlem, fully recovered, joined the conversation.

"Well, clearly she got to stay, " Harlem said as she daintily wiped the corners of her mouth, "Magdalena—"

"*Lady* Magdalena," she corrected sternly.

Harlem smiled courteously. "*Lady* Magdalena is in Harlem because she's colored, just like us. My grandmother—"

Magdalena's face flamed red. She slammed her palms on the table and roared. "I am *not* colored!"

"But..." Harlem stared at her. Perspiration sprang to her forehead and she felt like she'd swallowed a thousand burnt grasshoppers. "Are you sure? Because..."

"Quite." Magdalena gathered her composure and the pot of tea and walked to refill Harlem's cup.

Harlem looked at Ruth and Mary for some clarity. They offered none. "My. I'm terribly sorry. I thought—"

"No, you assumed."

"I'm sorry," she whispered. The room grew extraordinarily silent. The gurgle of the poured tea hitting Harlem's cup filled the room.

"Oh, you've gone over!" Harlem exclaimed.

Ruth grabbed the napkin from her lap, and although the table was far too large for her to help, she reached across the table to seemingly clean up the spill in front of Harlem. In the process, she knocked over Mary's tea cup, which created a cascade of tea on the maple table top.

"Whoops-a-daisy!" Ruth exclaimed.

Mary jumped up to avoid the tea spilling into her lap. She looked at Ruth, alarmed.

"Sister, it's a good thing that tea missed you," Ruth said.

"Yes, yes it is, sister." Mary's eyes softened in realization. She wiped up the tea angrily.

Magdalena was through with these people. It had already been a very long day and they were getting on her nerves.

"Tilda!" she yelled.

Harlem jumped in her seat. She turned toward Lady Magdalena, who stood in front of the office door she had closed earlier. She had her hands on her hips, looking very pinched and red and smoky, and that's when Harlem noticed it.

"Gee, that's something." She gazed at the enormous portrait of Lady Magdalena. It had broad strokes of color where there should have been fine lines and her form seemed to leap off the portrait like a ghost. In fact, her skin looked paler than it did in person. Quite like a ghost. Harlem stood slowly, using one hand on the table to steady herself as she tried to turn and get herself disentangled from the heavy purple chair that had seemed to grow into a straitjacket of vines. She wanted to look at this spectacle behind her full on. She freed herself and was face-to-kneecaps with the huge oil painting. She started to laugh.

"It's, it's—Oh my, I can't say what it is," she giggled as she turned back to look at Ruth and Mary to see if they were seeing what she was seeing. She plopped her bottom onto the table as she continued to stare up at the monstrosity.

Unable to resist, Magdalena turned her back to the portrait, raised her arm fashionably, thus striking its depicted pose. "A gentleman-friend mastered it for me in exchange for some services I provided him. I think he captured my true essence."

Mary snickered. Magdalena glared at her.

Harlem, still sitting on the table, groped for her teacup. Her mouth felt dry. She took a huge gulp hoping to quench the thirst. She set the cup down and missed the saucer. The cup tumbled to the rug-covered hardwood floor. It seemed too far away for her to reach it. Instead, she looked back up at the portrait.

"You look like a general. Like a non-colored general who has been out in the battlefield all day and he's been forced to now stand at attention for a very, very slow painter when all he really wants to do is use the ladies room very, very badly."

"*Tilda!*" Magdalena yelled again as she marched to her throne.

Harlem clamped her hands over her ears.

"Must you yell? We're all sitting right here." Harlem immediately covered her mouth. "I don't know why I said that…"

Only, since her mouth was covered, the words she was trying to say sounded like hollow mush in the chamber of her mouth. She turned her torso and gazed at the sisters, and then at Magdalena. Their faces started to blur into one another. Ruth's face jumped onto Mary's and then Magdalena's blurred between the two of theirs like a banana and peanut butter sandwich. She shook her head and felt her curls fall forward and stick to her forehead. She swiped at them with the back of her hand and was surprised by the dampness that was returned to her. Harlem instinctively wiped the wet from the back of her hand onto her dress. Then with her other hand, she sluggishly smeared the wet stain away as some twisted reminder that she was no longer the dirty girl Roy locked in the linen closet and wearing what may as well have been a sheet for a dress. She tried to lift her head in response to this reminder of her new stature, but couldn't. It wouldn't seem to rest on her neck properly and she felt it swaying from one side to another.

Harlem wanted to ask Ruth or Mary for help, or some kind of clarification on her current situation but her tongue felt thick as a cake of mud and wouldn't cooperate. Her legs were heavy. They wouldn't cooperate either when she asked them to hold her weight. As she fell forward, she succumbed violently and crashed to the floor in a sedated heap. Head first.

Tilda stood patiently by the doorway and watched the girl fall. This was her least favorite part of welcoming a new girl to the Manor.

HARLEM'S AWAKENING

CHAPTER 12

Tilda leaned against the door frame and waited for Mary to get away from the girl. She sighed heavily. It was Tilda's job to drag the girls away once they hit the floor. They'd all done this tons of times. But this time, Mary had run to the girl like it was suppertime and pushed Tilda out the way when she'd tried to get the girl. She wasn't goin' to fight Mary over no new girl, so she stood back and waited. And watched. What she really wanted to do was go to her room and cry long and hard. She didn't know how she was goin' to make it without Honey. She sighed heavily.

"She fell pretty hard," Mary said, as she felt Harlem's pulse, or at least pretended to do so. Tilda knew she wasn't feelin' for no pulse. She was trying to hide what she'd just stole. When Mary had rushed over, she went to where the girl was sitting first and flicked the girl's pocketbook onto the floor like it was some crumbs from the biscuits she made.

Mary shoved that thing in her skirt waistband behind her back while she bent down to act like she was real worried about the girl or something.

"Let's settle up, Magdalena," Ruth called out.

Tilda crossed her arms. Something was going on with these two. Usually they dropped off a girl, had a Sherry or two with Magdalena and then went off to wherever they stayed at night. This time Ruth and Mary barely talked to each other. Maybe it had something to do with this girl's handbag. Or what was in it.

Magdalena must have wondered too because as they paraded into her office, she noticed that the handbag was gone from the table.

Magdalena grabbed a biscuit and asked, "What's the hurry, Ruth?"

Tilda wondered why Magdalena would be concerning herself about Mary side-swiping a little old handbag. Tilda hunched her shoulders. *"What'd she care?"* Not much. Not much to care about now at all. Tilda snuck up on Mary and tapped her on the shoulder. Mary leapt up.

"My Heavens, Tilda!" she yodeled. Mary backed toward Magdalena's office door. "You watch her and make sure she's still breathing properly. Understood?"

Tilda kept her smooth brown face blank when they were ordering her around like she was somebody's dog. When she was with people she cared about, like Honey, she let her real self show and her real self was the one that felt things and cried and got mad. But, when she was with bad people like Mary or Ruth or Magdalena, she was blank.

Mary smiled big with her whole face and repeated too slowly, "Do you understand, Tilda?"

With her blank face on, Tilda scooped the girl by her armpits and began to remove her from the room. Like she was supposed to. Like she always did. Mary huffed loudly and retreated into the office. Tilda slowly dragged the girl out of the dining room, watchful she didn't leave a shoe behind, or worse. A girl's skirt slid right off, one time. Tilda tried to be more careful after that. She did her best to make this part as dignified for them as possible when she was carting them away, but it wasn't always so easy. She laid the girl down and pulled her soft skirt neatly over her white slip. She then hurried around and grabbed her by the armpits again and continued on.

"I wonder where she came from?" Tilda thought. She didn't know where or how the sisters chose these girls. Some of 'em looked a fright when they got to Magdalena's. But not this one. She thought this as she passed through the foyer toward the stairs. She'd already rolled up the oriental rug and moved it aside; she'd carted girls more times than she cared to remember and because of that, she knew that the rug always got in her way. A buckle in the girl's shoe would get caught on the fringe, and Tilda would be dragging the girl and the big old rug up the stairs. Or, it would bunch up and she'd trip over it and fall. One time she turned her ankle so bad, she could barely walk on it for weeks. So, she'd learned to quietly roll up the rug once Magdalena, Ruth, and Mary took the girls in the dining room. She'd also learned that when she heard the doorbell and Magdalena called out, *"They're back,"* that it was her job to get the biscuits from a tin in the kitchen (no matter how old they were), set the table quickly for four, warm the special tea, and tidy the dining room. Today, she'd also had to fix the chairs that Honey had knocked over when Otto dragged her out. She didn't like having to do that one

bit. Felt like she was crossing the arms on a dead friend in a coffin.

Sometimes, because Magdalena made her do things she didn't want to do, she found ways to get back at her. She'd bend her hair pins or drop an earring under her desk so she couldn't find it. Once she put a spider in her turkey sandwich, but then took it out because she wasn't sure if it was poisonous and if Magdalena died, she probably would, too. Today, to get back at her, she almost didn't fix the chairs back. She'd wanted to see how Magdalena would explain it to Mary, Ruth, and the new girl. She'd chickened out, though. She didn't want to get in trouble. It hurt when she got in trouble.

Tilda struggled to get the girl up the stairs. It seemed like the girl was getting heavier or maybe she was just tired. Or sad. Or hungry. There wasn't a lot to go around this morning at breakfast. It had been like that lately, and she always seemed to get the fatty piece of ham, the burnt piece of toast, or the last bit of scrambled eggs. Heck, if she'd known today was going to be her last breakfast with Honey, she sure woulda sat down with her and taken what she wanted.

As she turned to see how many more stairs she had to go 'til the top, Tilda decided that from now on, since she was the one doing all the cooking, she was going to start eating while she was cooking and not wait 'til somebody decided to offer her a scrap. Now *that* was a choice she could make! Tilda didn't feel like she had many choices. Especially when it came to living in or leaving the Manor. She'd been in that house her whole life. She didn't know nothin' else. She'd never been outside longer than it took for Magdalena to welcome in the new girl.

She'd learned some things from the girls that came in. She'd listen to them talk during the short time they were able to talk before they passed out. She'd hear where they were from: Kansas, Ohio, Kentucky, Alabama, Idaho... She heard these states but didn't know where they were or much else about 'em except how to pronounce them. These strangers brought in some of the outside, but nowhere near enough. She'd never watched the sun set or the moon rise, never felt the rain on her face or shoved her feet in the mud. She'd never thrown a ball against a wall and ran after it just to do it again. Never bought a stick of gum or sat and watched a picture show. Never sat at the window and looked at what was on the outside because Magdalena had all of the windows boarded up and covered with heavy curtains. Plus, all of the doors were locked, and even though she held the keys to each and every one of them, they basically led to nowhere.

She dreamed about leaving. Not really escaping, so much, but she dreamed of leaving. Peacefully. With help. Because, if she did get outside, say if she escaped or Magdalena threw her out, she wouldn't even be able to ask for help because her voice didn't work. In sixteen years, she'd never made a sound. Not even when she was a baby, Honey had told her. And no one knew why. Tilda thought maybe that was why her kinfolk left her on Magdalena's stoop. 'Cause she was defective.

Tilda pulled the girl to the top of the winding stairs. *"Good golly!"* she thought as she propped the girl's back against the wall. Tilda bent over with her hands on her knees and with her left leg she kept the girl upright. One time, when Tilda turned to unlock the door, the girl fell over and toppled all the way down the stairs. Tilda shook her little head fast and hard, trying to shake that memory out.

BING BONG!

She jumped straight up and had to reach for the girl before she fell over. The doorbell scared her every time. She waited. Magdalena yelled for her when she wanted her to answer the door and got it herself when she didn't. She hunched her shoulders. No yell. From her pocket she pulled the huge ring of keys that was always with her. Tilda unlocked and pushed open the door with her foot and quickly pulled the girl inside the room. It was sort of dark in there because the windows didn't work, as Tilda liked to call it. But she knew her way. There was only a bed, a valise stand, and a wooden chair in the room. A small bathroom was in the back. No need for nothin' else. 'Specially no dresser, 'cause once a girl made it to this room, she didn't belong to no clothes she brought with her and except what Magdalena gave 'em. And that wasn't much. Tilda had already put this girl's suitcases aside for Magdalena to go through. After she sprawled the girl onto the small rickety bed, Tilda plopped down beside her and reached for the high heel that had just sprung from her foot and toppled to the scratched hardwood floor. Not til she put her hand on her knee did she notice how bad it hurt. Lifting up her dress, a dried up bloody gash stared back at her.

"Poor Honey," Tilda thought.

"Momma!" the girl moaned.

Tilda pulled her dress down. Looked at the girl and tried to say it too, *"Momma."* Nothing. Nothing came out. She tried again. Her mouth moved like a gaping fish and her neck strained, *"Momma"* but no sound. Maybe she'd have been able to save Honey if she could scream or something. She

113

sighed. If her voice did ever decide to show up, Tilda thought her laugh might sound like purple, or her talking words would sound light and pretty like yellow, and when she spoke her name she'd sound like blue. But nothing had come out yet, color or otherwise. She was nothing. Grey. Like the sidewalk.

She fiddled with the shoe again. For a moment, she was thankful she was grey. At the Manor, being a grey sidewalk was safer than being a rainbow. Magdalena didn't sell sidewalks. She sold rainbows.

HARLEM'S AWAKENING

CHAPTER 13

BING BONG!

The doorbell rang again.

From the sliding doors, Magdalena yelled back, "Tilda! For Pete's sake! Get that!"

Tilda locked Harlem's door and began running down the stairs. Her little hand clung to the ridged banister for support. She reached the front door, unlocked it with the key, and barely had a chance to open it before Otto stormed through it and her.

"Where is she?!" he growled. His face was beet red.

Tilda tried to get in front of him to stop him, but with two fingers he sent her reeling across the floor.

"Magdalena!" he bellowed as he charged through the living room and into Magdalena's office with Tilda at his heels.

Magdalena looked up from her desk. She was counting bills out to Ruth and Mary, who sat in the chairs opposite her. Tilda ran into the room and stood behind Magdalena, pressed herself against the wall as she was prone to do. All eyes were on Otto as he threw a dress onto the desk

"That little harlot ran away!" he yelled.

The delicate flowered dress was torn down the front. It looked like an empty cocoon.

"Where's Honey?" Magdalena demanded.

"I just told you, she ran away!" Otto yelled. The thick veins in his neck popped like subway tracks.

Magdalena lifted the dress with her letter opener.

"Judging by that shiner on your eye, looks like she did more than just run," Magdalena said as she maneuvered the remnants toward Tilda, who quietly reached for the dress and hid it behind her back.

Otto's grubby fingers massaged the tattle-tale on his face. "Oh, I got her real good before I lost—"

"Lost?" Magdalena hoped Honey had enough chutzpah to take care of herself. "One of my girls is lost and running about in her underclothes in the streets?"

"You silly trollop," he spat. "Dees was not a part of d' deal. I want my money back."

Magdalena placed her hands on the bills. "Did you take a taxi, Otto?"

"I used up all my money on payin' for d' girl!" Otto roared.

"Otto. Your stupidity precedes you. I told you to take a taxi so that this very thing could not happen."

Otto pulled out his switchblade and pointed it at Magdalena. "I want my go'damned money back."

Ruth deftly grabbed a stack of money with one hand and with the back of her other hand, she made sure the little pistol she kept hidden in the waistband of her skirt was secure. Magdalena leaned into the desk and gripped her own pistol from its hiding place, which was under her desk beneath the sliding drawer.

"Let's be reasonable," Magdalena said.

Tilda backed into the corner, out of the way.

Otto was still standing behind Mary from her place behind Ruth's chair. In one swoop, he grabbed Mary and placed the blade against her supple neck.

"All of it," he said. "Now!"

Mary yelped, her eyes wide as could be. She turned to Ruth for help who tightly held onto the stack of bills as she stood. Ruth wasn't sure what to say, so she said nothing. She'd been in similar situations before, and she knew that sometimes keeping the mouth shut was the best initial defense.

"Ruth?" Mary's heart sank for the second time that day. She couldn't believe her sister did nothing. Otto tightened his grip, she winced and fought back tears.

"My boss ain't gonna like it too much I get back to d' docks with nothin'. You want 'em to come and do some damage or you wanna us t' handle it here on our owns?"

Magdalena released her pistol. He was right. She stood slowly, moved around her desk toward Ruth, and forcibly pulled the bills from Ruth's hands.

"Now hold on one minute, here!" Ruth said.

Magdalena remained focused on Otto as she walked back to her side of the desk, sat, and gathered the rest of the bills from the desktop. She took her time putting the money in an envelope. A drip of Otto's clammy sweat landed on Mary's forehead. Magdalena stared at the droplet as she slowly licked the envelope and sealed it closed. She placed the money on the edge of her desk.

"As you wish," she said.

Otto quickly released Mary, leaned his burly body over Ruth's vacant chair, and snatched the money. He backed out while wielding his knife and stuffing the money in his vest.

"Smart broad," he snarled as he ran out.

All three women released the breath they were holding. Their words tumbled into the office, neither really listening to the other:

"That Asshole!"

"He put a knife to my throat."

"I want our money."

"I coulda been killed!"

"Who the hell does he think he is? Lowlife, bottom-feeding—"

"You owe us, Magdalena—!"

"Killed! I coulda been killed!"

Tilda looked at Honey's tattered dress, listened to all of them sputterin' about themselves and felt like she was the only one that was wondering, *"Where the hell is Honey?"*

CHAPTER 14

Tilda tiptoed outside the office after putting Honey's dress in the closet. She leaned her back against Magdalena's portrait. She needed to think.

"Pay up!" Ruth said with such force, it seemed like the walls shook.

Tilda's thinking would have to wait. Tilda peeked her head into the office.

"You owe us. Now pay up!" Ruth charged.

Magdalena stood her ground behind her desk. "Your money just walked out the door."

Mary paced near the door while soothing her throat. "He was going to skin me alive!"

"Your lack of security ain't our problem," Ruth continued.

"And you did nothing!" Mary yelled to Ruth,

"I can't pay you what I don't have," Magdalena sneered. "His pay for Honey was going to be your pay for the new girl. We all know it is g-o-n-e, GONE! We're just going to have to chalk this one up as a loss for both of us, Ruth."

Ruth aimed her pistol at Magdalena.

"Oh, shit," Tilda thought. She welded her eyes shut.

"Our money. Now."

The bird acted as an alarm and started screeching and shrieking in its tiny cage. Tilda covered her ears.

"Shut up bird!" Magdalena shouted.

Tilda opened her eyes to see Magdalena pointing her own pistol at Ruth in what was now a standoff. Mary, seemingly oblivious to any of it, stepped between the barrels and cried to Ruth. "Do you really care about me so very little?"

"Mary," Ruth said while trying to stay focused on her job at hand.

Mary lifted Harlem's handbag to Ruth's face, blocking her view with it. "You care more about the money in this handbag."

Magdalena paused. "Money. What money?"

"Dammit, Mary! Keep your mouth shut!" Ruth said.

"What money, ladies?" Magdalena needled as she moved closer, still aiming her gun at Ruth.

Ruth tried to aim around her, while Mary threatened, "I'm leaving, Ruth!"

"Mary, you are in my way!" Ruth said.

"I don't care. You used to care about me, and I cared about you. It's over!" Mary barreled at Ruth.

"You've swindled us long enough, Magdalena! That handbag is my payback." Ruth hurled, stumbling backward toward the open door.

"Your payback? See, I knew it, Ruth. I knew it. It should be OUR payback!" Mary threw the handbag at her only sister and stormed out.

"Trying to cheat me, Ruth?" Magdalena asked, pistol aimed.

"Like you been doing me?" Ruth demanded. "Nice gown you're wearing. Is it new?"

"You're worried about a gown?" Magdalena laughed.

"What'd you have for breakfast this morning?"

From the dining room where she was watching, Tilda thought, "*Crummy eggs and burnt up toast.*"

"We had a tin of crackers. You're eatin' caviar and we're choking down crackers! When we started this racket years ago, you said we were going to be rich. Said we were going to change our lives and that things would be *won-der-ful*. Well, they are far from wonderful. For us. And I am tired of it." Ruth circled the desk. Magdalena backed away. "You, on the other hand, seem to be doing pretty well."

"And all this time I thought we were friends," Magdalena laughed wryly. She bumped into the bird cage as she circled. The parrot squawked.

"We were never friends. You were a tramp busted for selling yourself, remember?"

"And you were a stupid bumbling thief who couldn't steal a wallet without getting caught. And you're still just as stupid!" Magdalena grabbed the ashtray from her desk and threw it at Ruth.

Ruth felt the sharp sting of the heavy glass hitting her elbow, she screamed, "Owww!"

Magdalena lunged for the purse, but Ruth's ambition was stronger than her pain. Ruth ran and shouldered

Magdalena into the wall, scooping the purse like a loose ball on the field and plowing from the office like a football player.

Tilda scuttled for cover under the long dining room table as Ruth barreled from the office and into the dining room.

"That girl is my property now and so is that purse. You know the rules!" Magdalena charged after Ruth with her pistol drawn.

Ruth, two strides ahead, yelled, "Come and get it!"

Ruth threw a dining room chair behind her. Magdalena tripped over the chair, the legs of which became tentacles anxious to revel in the silk folds of the lustrous gown Ruth seemed to hate so much. As Magdalena tumbled, her finger squeezed the trigger.

From under the table and crouched on all fours, Tilda heard the loud pop and squeezed herself into a tight ball as she covered her head with her arms.

"*Jesus Christ!*" Ruth roared. She dropped to her knees. She felt like she was on fire. "My hand, oh my God, my hand!"

Tilda dared to open her eyes to make sure she heard Ruth right. "*Her hand?*" she thought. Turned out to be true, 'cause Ruth was up and stumbling around. "*Thank God. Thank God she ain't dead,*" Tilda sighed to herself.

Ruth felt dizzy; she caught her balance as she reached for the purse with her good hand. She could feel the warm blood seeping into her shirt as she held her burning hand close to her stomach, "*This is all Mary's fault!*" she thought.

Magdalena aimed the pistol at Ruth, "I would leave that if I were you."

Ruth felt for a chair to help her stand up. She didn't bother to point her pistol back at Magdalena. Harlem's money would be no use to her if she were dead.

"You go on and find your little sister. Take your shitty luggage with you. I never want to see you in this house again. You hear me?" Magdalena said, her words controlled by each breath as she lay flat on her stomach. Her elbows dug deep into the rug as she looked over the top of her pistol and aimed good and hard at Ruth's gut.

"You're going to be sorry for this!" Ruth yelled as she tumbled into the foyer. She gathered her suitcase best she could. Her stomach flip-flopped as she watched her own blood drip and splatter onto the hardwood floor She needed help fast.

"That'll be the day! You two-bit crook!" Magdalena untangled her dress from the chair's leg and pulled herself to all fours. She crawled toward the purse. She lay flattened as she opened the cause of their chaos and discovered the very large amount and gasped. "Greedy ungrateful bastards!"

Tilda flinched as the door slammed.

Magdalena finally noticed Tilda gaping at her from under the table. She pushed her dark hair from out of her eyes and snarled, "What the hell are you looking at?"

Tilda wasn't sure, so she shrugged her shoulders and shook her little head absurdly.

Magdalena pulled herself upright.

"Clean this mess up and get yourself together. And bring me that girl's suitcase!" Magdalena couldn't believe the beauty of the luck resting in her hands. It couldn't have come at a better time.

HARLEM'S AWAKENING

CHAPTER 15

Tilda hoisted Harlem's suitcase onto the gleaming table that trapped so many secrets underneath its shiny veneer, secrets that she often helped to make, unfortunately. When she polished the table, she'd often tried to release the secrets with each stroke, but hadn't been too successful.

Magdalena opened the valise. It was packed neatly with delicates and mementos that meant nothing to her. As she fiddled with a lace handkerchief monogrammed with "SM," Magdalena knew she was intruding just as any other thief, but this was her house and anything in her house belonged to her. There were rules, after all.

"Must I instruct you on everything, Tilda?" Magdalena said as she closed the suitcase. She was intrigued by its contents and wanted time alone with it. "Our guests will be here soon, we must prepare for them, no?"

Tilda was no dummy; she knew Magdalena was going to eat up the stuff in that suitcase just as quickly and messily as she did ice cream. Tilda left.

Magdalena pulled a diary wrapped in pink ribbon out of the girl's suitcase and cracked it opened like a leather-bound tomb. She turned the first weathered page and read aloud:

8, Jan 1926 - New York
Dear Child,

I've learned today that you are coming. I've only just married your father. He is sure to use this excuse to return us to Greensboro with my family and my family's money. His life is easier there. Mine shan't be. I've decided to name you Harlem so that I will always remember my life here.

Magdalena reviewed the check again. It was addressed to Harlem Winnepega Markeson.

"'Miss Smith', my ass!" Magdalena said.

Most of the girls Ruth and Mary brought to her were not of this caliber. Many of them couldn't even spell 'caliber.' She didn't always care about that. She cared about how they looked and how they spoke. Spelling could always be taught. Magdalena looked through the suitcase again before returning to the journal. She inspected a silver-framed photo of a striking, wistful woman who she assumed authored these musings. As she replaced it, she discovered some perfume in a dainty bottle nestled in the elastic pouch pocket. She dabbed it absently on her wrist and became intoxicated with lilacs and sage.

Magdalena closed her eyes involuntarily. A fragmented memory of her mother, Edith, materialized. Her round nose. Unyielding chin. Smiling, inquisitive eyes offset by skin that looked like it had been rubbed with roasted walnuts.

"Bad, bad juju in here, Maggie. Bad juju. Got to get rid of it before it can do anybody some harm," she'd say as she'd walk through their home with a burning stick of smoky, pungent sage. "Got to get rid of it."

Magdalena heard herself say, *"Yes, momma."* Burning sage to ward off bad luck or spirits had been a tradition passed down from her Haitian side of the family.

She rubbed her wrist roughly with a cotton shirt from the suitcase.

Got to get rid of it.

Was her mother speaking to her?

She felt stained. The journal would have to wait.

Tilda had wanted to see what was in the case, too. She'd hid behind the folds of the massive purple curtains that closed to hide the double sliding oak doors leading into the dining room. Tilda watched Magdalena toss the journal into the suitcase and hurry to the kitchen, near the rear of the dining room. Magdalena looked like she'd left some eggs to boil on the stove or missed the timer on a pot roast in the stove. But, Tilda did all the cooking; she couldn't imagine why Magdalena was behaving so.

Tilda slipped from behind the curtains, quietly slid the doors closed by their curved brass handles, and then drew the curtains. From the foyer, no one would never know a dining room existed. Once a new girl arrived, Tilda kept the doors shut and the curtains pulled, so that if a girl did escape her room somehow, she'd be disoriented and unsure of where she was and where she'd been. Tilda felt a breeze at her ankles. She bent to straighten the stretched cotton that pooled about her ankles like thick cream. She needed a new pair, but knew she probably wouldn't get some. She'd have to check the closet in Magdalena's office where she often threw the new girls' belongings. Maybe there would be a pair of socks there. Still hunched over, she spotted a few droplets of Ruth's blood. With her soft shoe, she rubbed them deep into the crevices of the wood floor and into a new secret. She then hauled the oriental rug back to its resting place to seal it tight.

She climbed the big old staircase. Her tiny shoes made no sound on the wooden stairs. She was quieter than a mouse. Always. Some people that visited the Manor never even saw her. But she saw them. Always. She had an advantage. She was small and there were many places to hide. Plus, folks treated her like a smudge on the wall: something out of place, something ugly, and something they hoped would go away. There was no reason for her to think of herself any other way. She *hoped* she'd be pretty one day. As for right now, her prettiness was like Christmas morning at The Manor: non-existent. That's why she smiled as she reached in her pocket and her little fingers played with the one thing from today that she'd kept for herself: the girl's lipstick.

Tilda dug past her private treasure to remove the huge ring of skeleton keys. They were heavy and because the cotton on her dress was far from new, at least one of the twenty sharp keys on the ring, whether it was a big one or a teeny tiny one, often found a way to make a hole in her pocket. She figured somehow it was their way of letting her know they were in charge, when really it was supposed to be the other way 'round. She knew every last place each one locked and unlocked, from the front door to drawers to cabinets to her own bedroom door, which was really the old broom closet under the stairs. The way she saw it, especially during those late nights when she was unable to sleep, she'd stare at the point her ceiling made and remind herself *she* was the real master of the Manor. Lady Magdalena could go jump in a lake. Tilda didn't have the voice or the gumption to tell her to do so, but she sure thought it enough.

Tilda got to the top of the stairs and passed Harlem's door, which was the first door. She knew the girl was still indisposed from the tea. She walked down the hallway past three more doors until she arrived at the fourth door. She fit its key into the lock and turned it quietly. The door swung open and Tilda stepped inside. It was dark too, just like the new girl's room, but this room had windows that worked half way. While the other rooms had windows that were fully boarded by wood that blocked out all the outside life and strangled the life inside, this room had windows that were only boarded from the bottom to half way to the top, so some life could come in. They'd tried to stand on the bed to see above the wood, but no one was really tall enough to look over the top part to see anything outside. Tilda moved to the dressing table. She ran her fingers over Honey's name which was carved into the wood around the oval mirror.

She pulled out the lipstick and turned it over in her tiny hands. *Iced Ruby*, she read silently.

Tilda peered at herself in the darkness. She saw a droopy stranger with thin cheeks, thick eyebrows and big round sad eyes. She decided to look at something nicer. She lifted up a tattered photo stuck to the mirror. A young girl holding hands with a mean looking white man with dark hair and bushy mustache, and a meaner looking colored woman with round cheeks and a small forehead, stared back. Tilda barely remembered them. These were Honey's momma and daddy. Honey had told her about them many times. She'd even said Tilda could pretend they were her own momma and daddy since nobody knew who hers were and probably never would know. She and Honey would make up stories and play them out in this very room and they'd act like a real family in those stories and Tilda would be happy and so would Honey. She loved Honey for that, especially since in real life, there wasn't no way those two people could be her parents, 'cause her skin was brown like the lady's and Honey's was honey colored… a mix of both of them.

Tilda looked at herself again. She'd have to find a way to be pretty without Honey now. She pulled out her necklace and let the "A" for Always breathe. She opened the lipstick. She'd seen Honey put some on before, but had never tried it herself. Her eyes nearly popped out her head when she looked at the lipstick, 'cause wasn't no lipstick there at all. There was money in there. All tightly rolled up and stuffed in the tube like a cork. She brought the tube up to her eyes real close to make sure she was seeing what she was seeing. It was money alright. Lots of it, too! She looked around real fast even though wasn't no one around to see her. She quickly put the lipstick cap back on and jammed the lipstick in her pocket that had the smallest hole.

"Well I'll be dammed," she thought.

CHAPTER 16

Harlem's tongue felt as heavy as the load of wet sheets Roy forced her to wash when he was through with her. Her head felt as weighted as her heart when she hung them to dry in the hot North Carolina sun. She wiped away damp hair that clung to her forehead.

"Momma?" she moaned.

Magdalena smoothed the hair from Harlem's face. "No, dear."

Harlem inhaled deeply. "Momma!" She shot up in the bed. Her eyes, once focused, saw not her home or her mother but Magdalena and Tilda.

"Oh, my. Hello," she warbled.

Magdalena sat next to her on the tiny bed. "How are you feeling?"

Harlem shook her head slowly and laced her hands over her face.

"Fragrance you're wearing. My mother wore the same."

Tilda watched a cloud sweep across Magdalena's face as she smelled her wrist quickly and then wiped it roughly on her thigh.

"She must have very good taste," Magdalena mustered as she offered Harlem the bottle of Coca-Cola she held. "Drink this, you'll feel better."

Harlem tucked her legs under herself as she leaned back into the wall with its wallpaper of tiny blue roses and drank.

"What happened?"

Magdalena smoothed her gown, which Harlem noticed was different. This one was a cascade of white silk that draped elegantly across her collarbone and shoulders, hugged her thin frame and finished with a flare of a short train.

"Exhaustion, I imagine."

"One moment I was looking at your painting and then...I...I don't know what happened after that."

"You fainted, we think," Magdalena crossed her legs demurely and straightened her rhinestone cuff bracelets about her thin wrists.

"I've never fainted in my life," Harlem said. She cooled her forehead with the chilled bottle.

"Well, there's a first time for everything." Magdalena stood. "Tilda took care of you. You're fine now."

"Where are Ruth and Mary?"

Magdalena pulled a long box from Tilda's arms. "They've gone off to the market. We needed a few extra things for tonight."

"Tonight?"

"It's my birthday!" Magdalena smiled grandly as she held the box.

"Oh dear," Harlem said. "Your birthday? No one said a word!"

"In all the excitement of your arrival and with you being indisposed, I'm sure we all forgot to mention it."

"Because your birthday was in April. It's June," Tilda smirked to herself.

Harlem stood on unsteady legs. "Well. Happy Birthday, Magdalena," she said as she offered her hand in celebration.

"*Lady* Magdalena, Miss Smith," she said as she shook Harlem's hand and then presented her with the large box tied with an enormous emerald-green satin bow.

"For me? On your birthday, Lady Magdalena?" Harlem removed the ribbon and lifted the box. She withdrew a sinful, garnet-red, crushed velvet gown, some silk stockings, and lace garters. "My!"

"Won't this look absolutely stunning on her tonight, Tilda?" Magdalena clasped her hands and said so without looking at Tilda.

Tilda nodded as she walked to the foot of the bed and opened Harlem's suitcase for her. Tilda had placed it and its match there nearly thirty minutes ago. The girl had been curled in a ball and hadn't moved a muscle, even when Tilda had put her ear near her nose to make sure she was still breathing.

Harlem's eyes widened. "Oh, I couldn't possibly. Tonight? My head is pounding, I've travelled so far. I really need to rest and…" She began to place the gown back in its box.

"Your first night in Harlem and you want to sleep? My dear Miss Smith, that won't do," Magdalena reached into the pocket of her gown. "Luckily, I anticipated this moment."

Lady Magdalena opened a tiny metal pill case and presented her with what looked like two small white pebbles.

"Benzedrine?" Harlem had seen her mother and Mrs. Whitscomber take them with their coffee. *To curb their appetite*, they'd say as she watched.

"You're saying I need to watch my figure?" Harlem said, lifting the dress. "I'm certain I can fit into this."

"Of course you can! What I'm saying is every girl needs a little pick-me-up. And these will do just that."

Harlem's mother often seemed happier and more energized after taking her doses. She'd smile from a faraway place and ask Harlem to dance with her in their studio. They'd *jeté* to the point of exhaustion, with her mother often taking a nap right there on the floor in their favorite room afterwards.

Harlem accepted the invitation to fly.

"Only because it's your birthday, Lady Magdalena." She swallowed them down with the Coca Cola as she prayed, *Please let this be alright!* She laughed nervously in return.

"I must look a fright. I'm certain with a bit more of a nap..." she said as she checked her Harvel watch of thin gold she'd picked out herself. Harlem bolted up in the bed.

"It is ten o'clock!" she exclaimed. "I've missed the entire morning."

"It's actually ten o'clock in the evening, darling," Magdalena corrected. "You were so, so tired."

"What?! You can't be serious," Harlem cried. "In the evening? I've gotten off to a horrible start." She quickly covered her face with the pillow, embarrassed. She dropped the pillow, smiled faintly, and stood. "Okay, let's get this show on the road."

"I imagine a hot bath will be in order?" Magdalena purred as she walked toward the tiny bathroom.

Harlem gasped as though she'd been punched. "No, thank you. A shower would be fine. I prefer showers." She stood and shook her head to release the vision of her mother's figure walking down their hallway.

"Suit yourself," Magdalena smiled as she stopped to gather the empty box. "We'll be back in ..."

Harlem stood in front of her open suitcase. "Who's been through my things?"

"Oh my goodness, it was me!" Magdalena rushed to Harlem and cradled her shoulders. "When you fainted, we tried to find any information we could. A phone number to someone we could call. We really made a mess of your things. Didn't we, Tilda?"

Tilda didn't like the word "we," but she nodded in agreement anyway from the doorway.

Harlem looked inside her pocketbook which had been placed inside the suitcase. The check was safe.

"Well. I can imagine it was a surprising time for all of us." Harlem nestled her pocketbook in the suitcase, gathered her toiletries, and turned toward the bathroom, "I'll be ready as soon as I can. I'm looking forward to celebrating with you, Lady Magdalena."

"As am I," she responded. "As am I."

HARLEM'S AWAKENING

CHAPTER 17

Harlem stood on tip-toe as she tried to check most of herself in the tiny bathroom mirror one more time. *"This is what it feels like to be beautiful,"* she thought as she turned round and round and allowed herself to smile at what she saw before her. She leaned into the mirror. Her nose crinkled. She wished she'd known better how to do her hair. Magdalena's had been swept into a stylish French roll that Harlem tried to copy, yet hadn't quite mastered. Her hands shook slightly as she made a final attempt at tucking her hair into a quasi-French bun. The pick-me-up had her jittery as did her nerves.

"Ok, then. It's an Italian bun!" she shrugged happily. Her hands flew to her stomach as it growled loudly. "Yes, a bun of any sort would be good right now, wouldn't it?"

Her stomach hadn't stopped growling since she'd stepped out of the shower. She pulled the chain to turn the light bulb near the mirror off and left. She walked quickly through her dismal quarters, while taking quick review. She pointed at the faded polka dot curtains that probably used to match the wallpaper.

"No." She spun in a *pirouette* toward her suitcase, closed it, pointed to the bed with its thin, white chenille bedspread.

"No!" She skipped toward the door giggling, as she then bowed deeply like a swan to the tall floor lamp with its silly, crooked, pale-yellow lampshade.

She sang in a loud Concerto Finale. "Noooooo!" Harlem laughed, "Tomorrow, the beautiful Ms. Markeson gets a new room!" She whisked open her door, pulling her velvet train out of the way as she glided gaily into the hallway.

Magdalena met her at the bottom of the stairs.

"I knew you would be stunning," she smiled as she took Harlem's hand and guided her through the foyer.

"My guests are excited to meet you," Magdalena said.

Harlem heard hearty laughter from the dining room.

"Me?" Harlem smoothed her dress. "I wouldn't know why."

"You must have more confidence, darling." Magdalena pulled Harlem to the dining room. "This will be one of the most memorable nights of your life."

They made an elegant, compelling entrance as they walked arm-in-arm into the dining room, which had been transformed into a ballroom. The grand table had been removed, and in its place were an assortment of gorgeous ladies decked in jewels and ball gowns, and sophisticated gentlemen clad in dress suits and tails who sipped champagne and spoke in dignified murmur under the low lights of the fantastic chandeliers.

"Ladies and Gentlemen! Please, Ladies and Gentlemen. I ask for your attention." The room quieted. Eyes of all sorts were upon them now. Blue eyes framed by round, wire-rimmed glasses. Hazel eyes set deep upon tanned, chiseled cheekbones. Dark-brown eyes offset by the smoothness of olive skin tones...

Harlem inhaled sharply. "I've never seen such a thing—"

Magdalena patted Harlem's arm reassuringly.

"Thank you all for coming to my soiree this evening. It is not often that I'm able to welcome such a beauty here. I'm just so honored she made it here in time for tonight's festivities. I present to you Miss Ann Smith!"

Magdalena stepped aside and with the rest of the guests, offered a welcoming cascade of clapping.

"I...I..." Harlem felt consumed by their stares.

"Just say 'Thank You,' darling," Magdalena said through a tight smile.

"Thank you, everyone. I....I'm pleased to make your acquaintance. Acquaintances. I mean, it's nice to meet you all."

"Bravo!" Someone yelled from a far corner.

Harlem felt the smile on her face grow until her cheeks stretched to its limit. Her hands flew to her cheeks to stop the grin from going too far. She curtsied awkwardly. "Thank you. Thank you!"

Magdalena linked arms with Harlem again. "Lovely job, lovely. Everyone simply adores you already. Aren't you so very happy you left Greensboro behind and came to New York?"

Harlem paused. "I am. But, how'd you know I was from Greensboro?"

"I went through your things, remember?" For once Magdalena told the truth. "Come. Meet my guests."

Magdalena released Harlem's arm as she placed her in front of a group of men.

"Oh, please. You musn't leave me."

"I'll be right back, Miss Smith. Introduce yourself." A man with a long face like a bloodhound pulled Magdalena away while staring at Harlem's speed bumps and hair pin curves which, against her will, fit quite seductively in the red gown.

Harlem bit her lip and wrapped her arms around herself as she stood before a horseshoe of men inspecting her. One looked like a handsome yet weathered scarecrow. Another had hair slicked back so neatly he seemed like an otter. Their eyes swallowed her like a glass of cold lemonade on a hot Greensboro day. She licked her parched lips.

"Pleasure to meet you all," Harlem said.

"You're a delight," one said as he drew closer to her.

"Thank you, sir." Harlem said, stepping back.

"Hello, dear," said a shorter white man with thick black hair and small black bright eyes that made him look like a rat. He stepped in front of the other man. "My name is Arthur Penn."

"Charmed, Mr. Penn." Harlem hesitated.

He reached for her hand. She scarcely lifted it from her side to offer it to him.

"Please, call me Arthur." He lifted her hand high and kissed it demurely, while looking into her eyes.

Her mouth dropped. He gently touched her chin and closed her mouth. "You're a long way from home, my dear."

"I guess I am," Harlem said. He smelled of freshly mowed grass and olives. He was that close to her.

"Please. Allow me to get you some champagne?"

"Champagne?"

"I see that you are a young woman, but certainly you've had your first champagne?"

"Yes, of course I have." She hadn't.

Arthur nodded and smiled broadly as he took a few steps, lifted a champagne from a passing butler, and gently gave it to Harlem.

"Drink. Please. Someone as divine as you should not be kept from whatever she desires," he said in a hushed tone.

"Thank you," she said as she sipped carefully. The bubbles tickled her nose and she smiled. "Sir?"

"Arthur."

"Arthur, I'm actually quite hungry. If you could get me something to eat, I'd be eternally grateful."

"Eternally? Well then, it would be my pleasure to comply!"

"His pleasure to comply?" Harlem thought as she took a larger sip. It had been The Turtle's pleasure to comply. Never in her life had someone like Arthur—whose entire generation thrived on people like her *complying*—had the pleasure of doing anything for her. She started to giggle again at the thought.

Arthur left her to retrieve some nourishment. He heard one of the men near Harlem utter, "Delicious," while another responded, *"Non, 'Delectable!'"* As he passed Magdalena, he handed her a small envelope prudently, while she in turn subtly removed a ring with a large baguette from her finger, which he placed on his pinky.

Finding a butler with hors d'oeuvres, Arthur selected some cheese and some wafer crackers. The sliced ham looked a bit putrid. He then plucked another champagne for Harlem. He flipped open the tiny hinge on the ring he'd just purchased from Magdalena. The Onyx baguette harbored a white powder which he emptied into Harlem's glass. He waited for it to dissolve before he rejoined his prey.

Harlem laughed heartily at something said in the group that had re-gathered in his absence. Arthur was certain it was drivel as some of these men were not as bright as they dressed up to be. In the past, only the elite were allowed at these soirees. Word downtown was that Magdalena was losing her footing here uptown and that someone was closing in on her. As far as he was concerned, this was the only place and the only moment in his secluded existence where he could get close enough to girls with mysterious, beautiful skin that trapped golden sunrays. So he would continue to come as often as his budget allowed, and his budget almost always allowed thanks to his father's steel corporation. He took Harlem's empty glass and gladly handed her the laced champagne and the light fare which he noticed had gotten even lighter from last month.

"You are such a help," she responded, still laughing at the spectacle before her. "Thank you!"

He rolled his eyes to the heavens and thanked the Lord for not blessing him with the height so many men coveted. At just 5'3 and a half, he was able to thoroughly enjoy the mole that danced enticingly on Harlem's ample cleavage as she laughed.

"Your wish is my command, dear." He smiled as he resumed his place by her side.

From across the room, Magdalena held court with another group of men and some women who buzzed around her like lustful bees. She watched Harlem and Arthur. "*She will do nicely,*" she thought with some relief as she absently massaged her aching knee.

"Excuse me, friends," she said and walked to the kitchen.

Magdalena reached just inside the kitchen door and pulled impatiently on a thin cord built into the wall.

Upstairs, in the bedroom next to Harlem's, a small copper bell above the door tinkled sharply. In response, three women gathered the trains of their sinful red garnet dresses and made their way to the party in the dining room below as they had done many, many times before.

HARLEM'S AWAKENING

CHAPTER 18

Harlem blinked again. She stared at Arthur. She swore he had just rubbed her back. She looked behind her and sure enough, there was his hand.

"Enjoying the party?" He rubbed her again. His eyes showered her with admiration.

Harlem moved away. "I am. Thank you."

Arthur moved closer. "As you should. As you should!"

Harlem fanned her face with her hands. "Is it warm in here?"

"Let's get you someplace more comfortable," Arthur murmured to her as he wrapped his arms about her tiny waist and steered her toward a chair off in a corner.

"I'll take good care of you, *mon cherie*," He kneeled in front of her as she sat. He caressed her face with his fingertips. "You're so beautiful."

Harlem looked into his eyes. She felt a little dizzy. Mouth dry. Her heart raced and her cheeks flushed crimson with excitement. She'd never felt this way before. He didn't look like the type of man to whom she would be attracted, but the hair on her arms told her otherwise. She could barely catch her breath. "Beautiful?"

He leaned in to kiss her full lips.

"No." Harlem turned her head, ashamed. "You musn't."

"Don't I please you my darling?" he asked.

She stood, pushing him away, when someone called out, "It's the Brown Betties!" Applause rippled throughout the room.

Harlem looked to where the crowd had begun to gather. And there, at the center of their attention were three breathtaking brown women dressed exactly as she was.

Harlem rose quickly. Arthur steadied her.

"Who are they?" Harlem asked. Her arm left Arthur's hold as she instinctively moved closer to the spectacle at the doorway. Harlem peered closely at the girls. Everything about them was like satin: the way they moved, their skin, their hair. She wrapped her arms about herself again and bit the inside of her cheek to ward off the sting in her eyes.

"You're just as lovely as they are, Ann. More." Arthur raised on tiptoe to whisper into her ear.

Harlem brushed him off with her shoulder.

"You musn't compare yourself," he said as he reached for her fingers.

She hugged herself tighter, shielding her fingers. "I'm wearin' the same dress, you dodo bird." Her voice worked to fight through the shards of disappointment lodged in her throat.

"Darling. What do you think of your surprise?" Magdalena appeared in front of Harlem, smiling smugly.

Harlem swayed on her heels and caught herself. "What do I *think*?"

Magdalena motioned for the three women to join her.

"These are The Brown Betties. I thought you'd be happy to learn that you were special, just like them." The women stared at Harlem.

"What kinda joke is this?" Harlem demanded.

"I assure you it is no joke," Magdalena circled behind the women and placed her long arms about their shoulders. "Right, Betties? Why don't you introduce yourselves to your new sister. Hurry now, we haven't much time. Arthur, dear, why don't you join me for a sip while these lovelies get acquainted."

The girls turned to one another, ignoring Harlem.

"What's she done with Honey?" Amoura exclaimed as her fingers flew to her pouty lips. Her almond-shaped, pale-brown eyes lit up with fear.

"Hello?" Harlem asked to their backs.

"This really had better be some kinda joke," Desire whispered as she hugged her slim yet curvaceous frame. She blinked her doe-like eyes, dark brown and pensive, and bit her rouged lip to stop it from trembling. "If Honey is gone. We're in trouble."

Fury turned to Desire, with round, nearly black eyes blazing. "We all know Magdalena doesn't joke." She stamped her foot. "God dammit!"

"One of you all want to explain to me what is going on?" Harlem demanded. She tried to put her arms on her hips but they slipped off. She timbered forward and found her cheek grazing Amoura's shoulder. The girls got her back to a vertical position.

"I got it! I got it!" Harlem cried, pushing them away. "Now spill it."

"Well, my dear. I don't know what you know and what you don't. But I'm gonna give it to you straight," Fury said. "First off, I'm Fury. Welcome to Lady Magdalena's Manor."

Harlem shook this girl's hand. She looked to be somewhere near her own age and was her height. The girl's grip was strong as was her chin. Her waved black hair framed her chestnut-colored face.

"I'm Ann Smith," Harlem responded softly.

"Girls, this here is the brand new Miss Ann Smith," Fury kicked at a nearby chair.

"And I'm Desire," the tall, thin one said. Her eyes were kind yet beguiling. "Despite everything else, we're pleased to meet you." She spoke with a clipped accent that sounded like someone from Chicago.

Harlem felt like she was looking at a model from a Macy's advertisement. But a brown one with skin the shade of cashews sporting a pixie bob.

"Pleasure, Desire," Harlem responded gravely. She was wilting in their beauty. She felt herself wanting to look at her shoes again.

"And I'm Amoura, sugar," the last one said with an accent Harlem found familiar. Harlem raised her head to see fine freckles dusted appealingly on Amoura's round face etched with the prettiest dimples and sparkling eyes.

"So," Harlem pitched slighty. "Now we know each other but I still feel like I been punched in the stomach. Ruth and Mary said I would love the girls here and that Magdalena — excuse me, 'Lady' Magdalena — would love me, too. Now, I want t' belong here. I want t' do that somethin' awful. But I don't know I want t' do it wearing the same dress as you all." Harlem's eyes filled. "That just don't seem fair. To me."

"Well." Amoura tilted her chin, touched her tight pin curls which clung attractively to her head and looked at Fury.

"Well—" Fury stopped, not knowing how much to tell. Desire shook her head. Fury took that to mean "take it slow" so she did.

"Go ahead. Give it to me straight, just like you said." Harlem looked at Fury.

"Okay." Fury began. "We are The Brown Betties."

"Yes?" Harlem furthered.

"We're a singing and dancing group here at The Manor. And, looks like by the way you're dressed, you're to be one of us, too." Fury finished.

"A Brown Bettie?" Harlem sniffed.

"Can you sing and dance, sugar?" Amoura said.

Harlem nodded.

"Well then, you're one of us." Amoura fixed her hair.

"One of us," Desire added as she smoothed her dress angrily.

The lights flashed three times and settled into darkness.

"Dammit!" Fury exclaimed again. "C'mon."

The room roared with excitement as the crowd threw their arms and top hats in the air.

"What's going on?" Harlem asked.

"Just follow us, Miss Ann." Amoura guided.

Six butlers with their white gloves, hired for these special nights, lit long tapered candles and formed an illuminated path which ran perpendicular to Magdalena's huge portrait. Magdalena stood proudly by the painting and pulled a thick, braided, gold rope hanging from the portrait. The portrait split apart and opened like the gates to hell, or elsewhere. The men whooped again and followed Magdalena, with Arthur by her side, through the portrait into an abyss.

HARLEM'S AWAKENING

CHAPTER 19

Harlem stumbled down the narrow stairway with the rest of the guests. Her hands followed along cool, smooth concrete as she tried to keep herself steady.

"Sugar, what did you take?" Amoura asked gently as they walked in the darkness with their gowns raised.

"I took some Benzedrine," Harlem hiccupped as she caught herself from falling.

"Bennies don't make you how you are now. What else?"

"Coca-Cola. Cheese. Arthur gave me some champagne—" Harlem recounted.

"Arthur. Right." Amoura said as she looked back at Desire and Fury.

"We'll just have to watch her on top of everything else," Fury said.

They finally reached the bottom of the stairs and were greeted by sultry floodlights which bathed luscious, gold curtains concealing a stage. A sensuous sign above, with tiny lights outlining intricate calligraphy, read: *LADY M'S MYSTERIE.*

"Well, I'll be a monkey's uncle!" Harlem exclaimed as she spun around. "A stage, in your own home?"

Desire pulled her by the arm. With her free hand, Harlem caressed the white linen which draped the crop of tables scattered throughout. Each table sprouted a single, delicate candle in a crystal holder. Harlem wiped the residue of tears from her cheeks. "I know you all are mad about something, but I do love to dance. Maybe, just maybe this is where I'm s'posed to be."

"We'll see how you feel about that in the morning," Desire said.

The girls lead her through the maze of tables and sat her in a chair at a center table.

"Don't move," Desire warned while pointing her finger at her.

"And don't drink nothin' else!" Amoura added. "We'll be right back."

"Wait!" Harlem yelled. "That girl you're lookin' for, Honey. Was she one of me. I mean one of you?" Harlem looked at them expectantly. Desire folded her arms. Fury turned her back. "I say somethin' wrong?"

"Honey was, IS, very much so one of us," Amoura ran her fingers through her hair. "Now sit tight."

Harlem watched the girls run off toward the stage and disappear behind it. She looked around at all the guests taking their seats and noticed a red curtain that ran the length of the cellar wall which curved into a large half-circle.

"So elegant..." Harlem exclaimed to herself. "Why would anyone want to leave?"

A butler passed with his tray of temptation. Amoura's instructions echoed in her head but she couldn't resist having another.

"Sir? Here please." She motioned. The butler, with his mocha skin and enticing eyes, leaned in as he placed the bubbly on her table.

"Hey there new gal. I'm lookin' forward to see what you got," he said.

"I beg your pardon?" Harlem recoiled as she covered her bosom with her arm, which is where his eyes had landed. Harlem looked around for Magdalena. Or even Ruth and Mary. She'd tell them what this man had said so that Magdalena could give her staff a speaking-to. Her mission was interrupted by the pleading call of a trumpet.

The gold curtains parted ceremoniously to reveal a trumpeter planted and silhouetted center stage. He loomed larger than life in the shadow as he wailed long and hard on his horn.

"Blow, Joe! Blow!" yelled a man close to her in a top hat.

The notes expanded and filled the room like huge soap bubbles. Harlem sat back in her chair with her mouth wide open. A booming, rippling cascade broke through the bubbles as the drummer sliced and diced the horn notes with his drum sticks. Joe, the horn man, moved from the shadow while more lights came on to illuminate the entire stage. Harlem watched the drummer dive into the ditty as his bowed head bobbed with each beat. Her heel tapped frenetically as it caught on to the next sound before she did. She thought about the jumpin' Brownstone from earlier as she leaned forward with her head cradled in her hands to watch the fluid trail of the bass man's fingers as he journeyed up and down the neck of the bass. Her head slipped off her hands unwillingly. The room turned sideways but when she righted her head back on her hands, everything was fine. When the wave of the clarinet crashed in and ribboned through all of it with its siren call, Harlem couldn't help but clap again with joy that had so quickly and ecstatically washed over her.

"Bravo! Bravo!" She shouted in admiration as she clapped and clapped while standing looking round at the other tables. Some folks were feeling as euphoric as she was starting to feel, while others happily puffed on cigars and nodded in harmony with whichever part of the experience spoke to their being. She blinked several times. The chairs kept leaping from one side of the room to the other. She steadied herself on her table with both hands and plopped into her chair.

Desire, Amoura, and Fury filed back into the room and joined her.

"My head is pounding," Harlem said. "One minute I feel...and the next I feel something else."

"Hush, Ann," Amoura guarded as she blotted her eyes with a corner of the table cloth.

"What's the matter, Amoura?"

Amoura spotted the empty champagne glass and threw her arms in the air. "I told you not to—oh, never mind," she cried.

"Okay. Let's face facts, girls. We know now that Honey is gone. Tilda confirmed it. What're we gonna do?"

"Hey, lemme ask you something. Why would Honey wanna leave all this?" Harlem asked.

Fury rested her elbow on the back of her chair, cradling her head. "That's the problem. She didn't," she grieved aloud.

A tear attempted to spring from her eye and she stopped it cold with a heavy swipe.

The music slowed to a tempo much less rousing and Harlem felt the crowd settle back in their seats. She saw the crowd's eager profiles.

"These folks look like they're waiting for a warm pie to come out the oven," she thought. She turned her gaze to the stage and allowed herself to be served.

Magdalena sauntered to the stage. The crowd clapped their gloved hands with polite sophistication. Her white gown glowed in the seductive light.

"Ladies and Gentlemen, I welcome you to *Lady M's Mysterie*," she soothed. "Where your heart's desire is delivered to the palm of your hand! I present what you've been waiting for. The *mysterie* that makes a performance show at Lady M's like no other. I present the first act tonight. The Rainbow Girls!"

She majestically stepped aside as seven women of various shades of brown, yellow and white sashayed onto the stage like lightening. The band switched into a staccato number that had the girls kicking high and fast with long legs that seemed like satin ribbons. Crimson mouths smiled below masquerade masks, each a different color of the rainbow. Purple fringe bounced and bobbed from low cut, shiny satin bodices which had far less fabric than the swim wear Harlem wore when she dipped in the creek. She wiggled her toes and felt the cold water on them as she closed her eyes and her mind took her back home.

Arthur leaned forward onto his elbows and dipped his finger in the growing pool of hot candle wax; he rolled it between his fingers as it cooled. His beady eyes glowed in the candlelight as he watched Ann's chin drop to her chest. Her hair fell about her ears, which Amoura quickly remedied. Whatever Magdalena gave him had finally worked. He studied each of the other girls at the table. He'd as of yet not enjoyed any of the other girls in red, The Brown Betties. The second act for tonight. They were out of his league. *La crème de la crème.* He locked eyes with Fury. She spit venom at him with her gaze. He retreated, for now.

He turned his shoulder to their table and watched the seven women ooze into the audience of bankers, politicians, authors, and such. Nowhere in Harlem, or elsewhere as far as he discovered, could a man such as himself enjoy this type of evening. No place was as risqué; no place was as exotic; no place knew how to please it's clientele with something they had never seen before. He'd been to The Cotton Club; tea and cookies as far as he was concerned. Hell, a colored girl couldn't even dance on the same stage as a white girl over there. He pulled up his tuxedo pant, crossed his leg and enjoyed.

The girl in the green mask rubbed Mr. Trieg's leg with her milky thigh, which was nestled neatly in a silk stocking held up by two delicate garters. Mr. Trieg's face flamed as it always did; Arthur would meet with him at the bank on Monday and neither of them would mention this. The girl in the purple mask sat sideways in Mr. Clarke's lap, leaned back, and stretched like a minx so that she also lay in the lap of Mrs. Clarke seated right next to him. The girl turned onto her stomach so that both could playfully tap her plump beige bottom. Both Clarke's giggled with excitement. They were new. They owned a bakery on 41st street and were prone to give free bagels to those they recognized from Lady M's. He'd see them on Tuesday. Arthur turned as he heard a loud guffaw. It was Mr. Yoo. The girl in the blue mask had taken his hands and slid them up her hips past her midsection along the sides of her torso, which Arthur could see gave Mr. Yoo a feel of her large distractors without really touching them. Mr. Yoo was the one who introduced him to Lady M's.

The rest of the four girls were in similar states of enticement as Arthur surveyed the room. His brow perspired in the candlelight. He removed his top hat from his head and placed it in his lap as his pants had begun to rise in a way that embarrassed him. These Rainbow Girls were a delight, but none of them held his attention as much as the new girl. He spied on the sleeping Ann Smith from afar. Waiting for the opportunity to have her. Hoping to be the first with her. Nothing was guaranteed at Lady M's. He'd been disappointed before, but prayed this time he would not.

The band stopped. A tom-tom beat summoned the women back to the stage in a frenzy that reminded him of the Can-Can dance. From the stage, their chests heaved as they caught their breaths. Red mouths plastered with wide smiles. They turned slowly with their backside to the audience; mechanically crisscrossed their arms about one another, just like the Can-Can and stood quite still.

Heads bowed as the ladies and gentlemen of Lady M's Mysterie drew to the dim light offered by the flickering candles. Their pencils scratched feverishly on paper Tilda had placed at each table hours ago.

Magdalena emerged from the shadows and quietly gathered the cards. She walked to the wall near the far right of the stage, grabbed the edge of the red curtain, and like a ring leader, she slid the curtain as she walked. Metal rings scraped against a metal rod. One by one, the curtain revealed seven doors, each the brilliant color of the rainbow. Red. Orange. Yellow. Green. Blue. Indigo. Violet.

When the scraping stopped, the women bent over. Their purple roundness punctuating the stage. Arthur felt his colleagues sigh with eagerness. He felt someone kick his chair. He looked over his shoulder. Lucinda winked and blew a smoke ring at him from her cigar. Her pale blue eyes danced against her darker features as she smiled broadly. She liked to play dress-up and today she was in a pin-striped zoot suit with her hair slicked back. She somewhat resembled the film star Greta Garbo.

"When am I gonna see you over at my place, Arty?" She chided.

Her place didn't have what Magdalena's had. "Soon, Lucinda! Soon," he chummed.

"Soon ain't soon enough, Arty. You catch my drift?" she smiled as she leaned her chair back on two legs. Her two-tone black and white loafer kicked his chair again.

Magdalena arrived for his card. "I imagine I already know your bid, Arthur?" she said demurely as she touched his shoulder.

"That you do," he responded.

"Hey Maggie," Lucinda blurted. She pounded the chair forward. Her elbows rested on her knees. Lucinda was an only child and acted like one.

"Lucinda, darling!" Magdalena said as she approached her.

Lucinda pulled her by the arm down to her level. "Don't *darling* me," she sneered. "We're due for a visit, wouldn't you say?"

"Things have been slow, Lucinda."

"Is that so?" she said as she looked around.

"Yes...tonight, is a fluke," Magdalena said as she fell forward and caught herself with her hand on Lucinda's knee.

"A fluke? Ok. Ok. I see. Your side business is still lucrative, isn't it *zeeskeit*?" Lucinda said as she drew on her cigar.

"Not as much—" Magdalena winced as Lucinda dug her nails into her arm and blew the smoke at her.

"Otto tells me differently." Lucinda breathed into her ear.

"Shall I come over tomorrow?" Magdalena didn't wait for an answer as she jerked her hand away from Lucinda's.

"We'll have cocktails," Lucinda released her grip. "And we'll talk about who really owns this place."

Fury watched Lady Magdalena return to the stage. She seemed caged like the bird in her office. She smiled slowly as she sat back and crossed her arms.

Magdalena rubbed the indent in her arm from Lucinda's nails as she reviewed the cards. *"That God-damned Lucinda!"* She thought. *"I own this fucking place. I earned it. It's mine!"* She turned and faced her audience. Her hands shook in anger as she pulled the first card and deliberately smiled brightly as she addressed her patrons. *"Monsieur Onze: Bleu!"*

Sapphire, the girl in the blue mask, stood upright and faced the stage. From behind her mask, she watched "Mister Eleven" step onto the stage, hand Magdalena a thick envelope, and reach for her hand. It was Mr. Yoo. It was always Mr. Yoo. He escorted her to the blue door. As they entered, Sapphire heard Magdalena call out the next. *"Monsieur Vingt-Deux: Rouge!"*

Ruby in the red mask, hesitated ever so slightly as she stepped forward for Mr. Twenty-Two. Magdalena pushed her forward. Ruby's hand shook as she extended it for the man to take it. As she neared her door, her knees buckled.

"Let's go, sister," the man whispered as he caught her. Her stomach lurched, and she was certain she was going to vomit.

Magdalena made a mental note as she watched Ruby falter. She called out the next, *"Monsieur Trois: Vert."* She smiled faintly at Mr. Clifton as he led Emerald, the only girl with blond hair, to the green door.

Arthur watched Mr. Yoo disappear into the blue door. *"Lucky devil,"* he laughed. Mr. Yoo always chose Sapphire; everyone knew to not even bid on her anymore if he was in attendance. Mr. Trieg nearly skipped his way to the orange door. A new fellow held the door and bowed as Indigo stepped into hers. The Rainbow Girls were all nearly spoken for. Arthur hadn't bid on any of them today. He waited patiently for something else.

Magdalena slid the remaining cards into her pocket. She glanced at Harlem, who was still passed out with her head nestled in her arms. She turned to Topaz, the yellow girl, and whispered, "Today is your lucky day, honey." Tears of relief tumbled below her mask as she turned and walked off stage.

"Heeeeyyyy! What's the big idea? What about the yellow girl…?" someone called out.

Lady Magdalena smiled pleasantly, ignored him, and signaled the butlers to return with more cigars and champagne. As she did so, the band mixed the colors of the rainbow into a swirl of red hot jazz with Joe taking center stage again. He pressed the cool metal to his lips and blew into the trumpet until he forgot his name. With his eyes squeezed shut, his mahogany fingers saw everything he needed. When he finished his solo, he opened his eyes, smiled at Desire which made the apples in his cheeks grow.

His kind eyes looked into hers; he winked and summoned her as he began to play her number.

From her chair, Desire nodded to Joe subtly, and began. She lifted her arms slowly as though her lover were removing her slip over her head.

"Here we go," she whispered to the girls as she rose from the table, stood tall and on pointe for all to see, before she fell forward and whipped and undulated her body through Joe's notes and then through the tables toward the stage as cunningly as an eel. Amoura slid her curvaceous bottom onto the table, released her spine to the table, arched it with suppleness that matched the blues from the clarinet, and with her head thrown back, she kicked her legs through the slit of the velvet gown as it fell deliciously against her waist revealing shapely legs that any man would want wrapped around him. She sprung forward out of the arch, sashayed from the table, grabbed a top hat, and placed it playfully on her head as she spun like a top toward the stage.

When the drummer boom, bam, banged, Fury whipped her torso toward her chair, stabbed her foot into the seat while flicking her dress back like a Matador to reveal a garter, which she snapped seductively. She spun back around, dropped to the chair, and scissor-crossed her legs into a wide "V" faster than the drummer could bang out his next beat. She pranced to the stage where the girls then danced in steamy precision. They swirled their hips so that the red velvet mesmerized the crowd into a soothing trance. They dipped their shoulders, whipped their heads, and elongated their legs like pulled taffy and intertwined their arms like twisted licorice. It was hard to tell where one woman ended and another began until Amoura unzipped Desire, who unzipped Fury, who spun and unzipped Amoura...and in a flash, with a final magical plead from Joe, their dresses dropped.

Lucinda sent a piercing whistle through the room. Arthur looked back at her admiringly. He merely cupped his hands about his mouth and hollered. The Clarkes stomped their feet and pounded their fists on the table like chimpanzees.

Arthur loved this part of the show. The girls shimmied in panties and push-up brassieres that plumped their distractors scrumptiously. Their undergarments were blanketed in silver sequins that shot fireworks into the crowd each time the light caught the shimmy. He'd gone to several department stores all over Manhattan looking for their lingerie and couldn't find it anywhere. He'd ask Magdalena tonight if the girls made these heavenly pieces themselves. He saw her standing next to Officer Brighton, the big lug who took care of security. They were posted at the bottom of the stairs which lead them all from the ballroom down into the Mysterie Club. He joined both of them there as Amoura, Fury and Desire continued to sizzle on stage.

Magdalena nodded formally as he approached. "The yellow door is vacant, *Monsieur*," she said.

"And I will gladly occupy the vacancy, Madame," Arthur nodded back as he removed two very full envelopes from his suit jacket.

Officer Brighton nudged Arthur roughly with his elbow, "I'll be gettin' your luggage, there, Mon-sir."

Arthur smiled casually at Brighton's attempt at French.

"Ain't it great doin' business wit' your own kind? I gotta deal wit' the darkies at the speakeasy over on Lenox. But over here," he looked appreciatively at Magdalena and Arthur. "We's all the same."

"Watch for my cue, *mes amis*." Magdalena departed swiftly.

The girls were nearing the crescendo of their act. Officer Brighton jabbed Arthur again. "Here it comes. Here it comes!"

"Yes, I know." Arthur grimaced and rubbed his rib.

With sophisticated expertise, the girls unclasped their brassieres and flung them into crowd as they playfully covered themselves with their arms.

"Just once, I'd like 'em to slip with them there brassieres and see the bongos," Officer Brighton chided. "You know what I mean there?"

Arthur pretended to tie his shoe so that Brighton's chummy meat chop hit air instead of his back. "Yeah, I know what you mean there," he mumbled.

Magdalena stood center stage as Amoura, Desire, and Fury walked backwards while smiling cunningly and turned their bare backs to the audience to wave "goodbye" with both arms in the air. Arthur heard Lucinda whistle again.

"La crème de la crème Messieurs et Mademoiselles! The Brown Betties!" Lady Magdalena bellowed. The crowd jumped to their feet and cheered appreciatively. *"Qui voudrait d'un ménage a trois?!"*

The men used their fingers to bid. Mr. Rathbourne, a looming Wall Street man, held up all ten fingers triumphantly. He was in a league of his own tonight. Lady M nodded to him; with his long legs, he arrived at the stage in two strides, it seemed. Amoura, Fury, and Desire disappeared through the curtains backstage and Mr. Rathbourne followed gallantly for all to see. But, what happened backstage, what everyone didn't know, was that Mr. Rathbourne would be given a champagne laced with

Magdalena's opium and arsenic and he would fall quickly asleep and wake up in a position that made him think he'd had a *ménage a trois.*

"*Merci* Ladies and Gentlemen! *Merci* and *Bonne Nuit.* Thank you and good night!"

Lucinda blew Magdelna a kiss and laughed while grabbing the arms of her chums. Magdalena pretended like she didn't see her and waved gaily to no one in particular.

The band played an exit tune as the well-heeled and well-rounded murmured about the night. Mr. Trieg jaunted from his orange door, pounded his chest, and whooped like Tarzan. Arthur winced in disgust. It was men like him that brought this place down.

Officer Brighton gently scooped Harlem into his arms and followed Arthur to the yellow door. Arthur salvaged a candle from a nearby table and quaintly held the door for Officer Brighton as he laid her on a simple, low cot in the very narrow, dark room. Arthur reached in his pants pocket for the small roll of bills he reserved for this moment and handed it to his accomplice who backed away soundlessly. Arthur smiled grotesquely while placing the candle on the floor near her head so he could see her beautiful face and intoxicating skin. He was so hungry for her. He quietly closed the yellow door.

And the band played on....

CHAPTER 20

Harlem stared at a ceiling she couldn't see.

Sorrow seeped from her eyes like putrid sap and glued her to the bed while the darkness covering her was a deadened sheet of lead. Trapped beneath its weigh, the only thing that moved was her breath as it tip-toed through her body as though not to wake the anger that lived constricted in her blood.

Roy had visited her. Only Roy was dead. It had been someone else. Someone who smelled of pine and cigars. And sweat. She was wrapped in his scent and it was strangling her with its power, which was knowledge. It had been present when she was not. The scent knew its owner and how, and when, in what ways, and for how long he came to have knowledge of her body. She felt the scent touching her, holding her, moving about in her insides. She struggled against its grip, its weight, its memory. It laughed at her as she began to thrash against its hold. Laughed the way Roy did when she'd ask him why he couldn't stop doin' what he was doin'.

Her breath was now sprinting, chased by anger.

"Why!" she wailed from the place deep within her where the scent was using its crow bar to rip open the coffin box she'd only nailed shut less than a day ago. It tore through the box, releasing every bit of her that had been concealed there: the screeching bed springs, the clinking chandeliers, the shame, the guilt, the red water of her mother's last bath, the stinging, the burning, the wishes to die. She screamed and writhed in the bed as each bit that made her who she was and didn't want to be grew and multiplied like the plague and tore through her with no mercy. She pleaded "Why!" again and again. The question piercing the darkness, each time louder than the scream before so that it began ripping her voice from her throat and throwing it against the bare wall like how her grandma killed defenseless rats on the farm.

In the next room, Tilda, Amoura, Desire, and Fury sat helpless on the splintered floor around the glow of a candle. They were draped in pale, thread-bare lingerie that hung loosely from their bodies. Their shadows danced sadly against the wall as they shared a cigarette between them. Tilda, always in her cotton dress, rested her head in Amoura's lap while she toyed with Harlem's lipstick of money. She rapped her knuckles lightly on the floor. *"She alright?"* she asked in the Morse Code Amoura taught her, that was only used between the girls. Amoura brought the cigarette to her lips, wincing at Ann's horrific howl in the next room. She released a cloud of smoke, hoping it took some of her sadness with her.

"She's gonna have to be, sweetie pie." She passed the cigarette to Desire who drew her knees to herself and put her head down. Fury took the cigarette, wiped a tear from her cheek and inhaled deeply.

Harlem buried her face in her pillow, hoping to suffocate her pain, to help it along as it worked to kill her. Pulled tight into a ball, she felt the velvet on her legs. It was a witness. An accomplice to the wickedness that had followed her from Greensboro and to which she now truly believed she deserved. She sprung from the bed and fell into a heap on the floor. Her breath rasped sickeningly through her body as she tore herself from the confines of the red dress. She kicked it from her and beat it with her heels and then her hands as it was the only thing she could blame.

Dragging herself to the bathroom, she wanted to purify and release herself from the scent which tormented her along with everything else. As she reached the cold tile of the bathroom and pulled herself up to the tub, she wished she'd been smart, like her mother.

Nearing 10 years in Los Angeles via New York and Chicago, Peppur has seen success as a writer, producer, actor, dancer and singer. As a playwright, Peppur has written *Harlem's Night Cabaret* performed by The Brown Betties (dinner theater), *The Build UP* (site-specific theater), *Dick & Jayne Get A Life, House Rules,* (full-length stage plays), as well as *Flapjacks & Orange Juice* and *I See*, both one-acts.

Peppur's non-fiction essay, *Three-Way* appears in Ava Chin's *Split: Stories from a Generation Raised on Divorce*. She wrote a book of short stories based on her first two years of living in LA, titled, *Making Lemonade: Bittersweet Tales from an Actress Being Squeezed in LA* and has a column in *Humor Mill Magazine*.

While in Chicago, she performed for thousands as a World Champion Chicago Bulls dancer and sites this experience as a turning point in making a beeline ascent toward her dreams. The Marquette University graduate and Kenosha, Wisconsin native is determined to further her career in her LA surroundings.

Lilliam Rivera is a freelance writer and editor whose work as appeared on E! Online, *California Apparel News*, Stylenetwork.com, *Latina*, and as the editorial director of lifestyle site Mondette.com. She's a 2013 PEN Center Emerging Voices Fellow and a 2013 Enchanted Land Fellow at A Room of Her Own Foundation. Lilliam lives in West Hollywood with her husband and two daughters and spends her time writing young adult novels and short stories when she's not procrastinating on twitter @lilliamr.

Benjamin grew up in the green hills of Gloucestershire in the west of England, before studying Illustration at the University of Brighton. Now encamped in north London, he works as a freelance illustrator for editorial, advertising and publishing clients. He still misses the countryside, and can often be found exploring London's pockets of urban woodland.

7505581R00109